The X Series:

Tenochtitlan Must Fall

by Gabriel Hugo

I0674499

Mission, Tx

Tenochtitlan Must Fall

(The X Series)

Editor, Book Design & Graphics by G.H.S.

Front and Back Cover Art designed by G.H.S. with
original art and works in the Public Domain. For
specific sources go to gabrielhugo.com.

Review of *Tenochtitlan Must Fall*

"*Tenochtitlan Must Fall*, book 1 of the X Series by Gabriel Hugo, involves the reader in a world of simultaneous dreams. In reading we meet Tonali, as a young boy and as an adult, who lives in a Mexico at the end of the fifteenth century. We experience this character's rite of passage from boy to man while we discover the political entanglements that existed in pre-Hispanic Mexico.

Deftly Gabriel Hugo weaves parallel realities that describe Tonali's Mexica-Aztec life: first suffocated by the impossibility of a real change in his life, then as pochtecatl-merchant, traveler and spy for the Mexica-Aztec empire; of his first love, of their family life, of the different indigenous worldviews, of the cultural and linguistic diversity of that pre-Hispanic Mexico, and of the circles of power that surround it.

Reading *Tenochtitlan Must Fall* is like sampling the waters that flowed in the canals at the center of the world, Tenochtitlán: saturated with history, with details of daily life, and with emotions that invite the reader to not abandon its pages."

-Xanath Caraza, author of
Hudson

This story is based on true events.

For more background information prior to reading, go to the "Addendum" at the back end of the book.

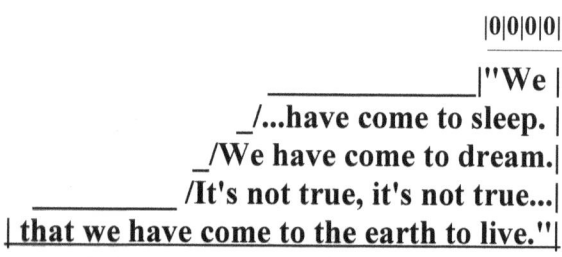

```
                                        |0|0|0|0|
                                        _____
                        _____|"We |
                        _/...have come to sleep. |
                        _/We have come to dream.|
                _____ /It's not true, it's not true...|
        | that we have come to the earth to live."|
```

-Fragment of Anonymous Nahuatl Poem

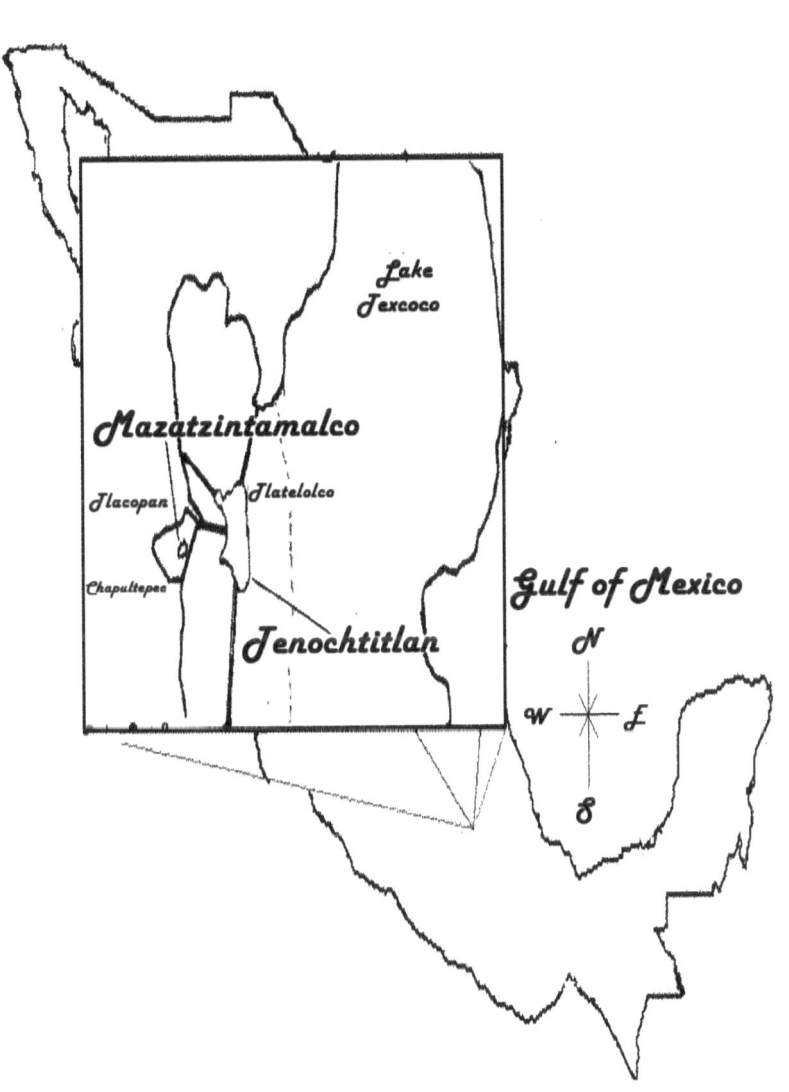

Table of Contents

(0)

On October 23, 2017, while playing in a cave at the top of the hill of Tarengo in the little town of El Tarengo Nuevo of the municipality of La Barca (a.k.a. Villa de Garcia Marquez) in the state of Jalisco, a young Mexican boy discovered a stone box wrapped in layers of tightly knit agave fibers. Months later he would tell reporters that he knew it was ancient simply by the condition of the materials used which easily broke off as he unwrapped. Nonetheless, he had been so curious as to the contents that he fought his natural instinct to take it to an elder for first inspections.

The contents in the box was a 23-sheet codex written using Nahuatl glyphs, the Nahuatl language using the Latin alphabet, and Spanish. Although the claims of fraud were quick to take to the airwaves, the codex appeared to most observers as legitimately dating to the sixteenth century, apparently having been written shortly after the fall of Tenochtitlan. The following is a partial English translation of the manuscript. Some passages, phrases, and terms have been added in areas of the codex where time and the elements have eroded the original completely, rendering it illegible.

Document 1521-X23
Source: National Institute of Anthropology &
History (INAH), Mexico City (CDMX)
Codename: X Codex
Investigation: Chicana/o Studies Institute,
University of Texas Rio Grande Delta (UTRGD)

Transcribed and translated as follows:

"Between dreams and waking lies the full potential of nothingness." That was what a voice in my head said to me one night before I slipped into the hands of the dream gods. I didn't know what it meant. How could nothingness be of any value? Possession seemed far more profitable in my young mind's view. After all, you can't buy anything with nothing. Nobody ever does anything for you for nothing. It was pretty clear to me that nothingness had no value. That was the philosophy which I had followed for a long time since my childhood. That is, until I discovered what the true value of nothingness really is.

It's nothingness that allows for something to appear. One must have an empty stomach in order to hunger for food. One must be without drink in order to thirst for water. One must lose oneself in order to find oneself again. And as a collective, a people must lose a nation in order that they create a new one. In that sense we really are like the gods of creation. We've always known from our teachers and our priests that life is cyclical. The earth itself has been destroyed several times already. Had it not been so, our fifth sun in which we currently live could not have been born. Now I understand the true meaning of nothingness. It is not the absence of that which is of value. It is precisely the condition which assigns value to everything that comes into being. In that way, it is the most valueable condition in existence. Nothingness is not destitution, but the richest form of having. It is the true fulfillment of destiny. In no other certainty of life is this truth manifested more perfectly as in the fact that all things that come into being sooner or later cease to be. Man, beast, flower plants, or nations all rise and fall.

It is daunting, no doubt. I am scared now in my old age. Only because of the uncertainty of what lies beyond death. But if the world of the living has taught me anything it is that no matter how tragic the sudden change to our comfortable existence might be, it always carries the full potential of nothingness. Death, therefore, is the opportunity to be reborn mightier than ever. Perhaps we will be reborn as gods. But before I meet my destiny, I wish to sooth your fears, my children. Dry your tears and listen up as I tell the story of the fall of the great Tenochtitlan. Nothing has been lost. We have gained much.

I was only nineteen years of age, curiously, also on a deathbed. In my convalescence, I journeyed back and forth between the land of dreams and waking. In my travels, I visited the days of my childhood and the circumstances which formed the man I was to become...

3

While I was sleeping...

I am running up the man-made hill on the outskirts of my neighborhood. We live on the western side of Tenochtitlan on an island called Mazatzintamalco near one of the two causeways leading to Tlacopan. I get to the top of the small hill we call "Little Chapultepec," a reference to the actual site further down south along the mainland shore of the lake. Little Chapultepec is the result of several generations of immigrants carving out chinampas and neighborhoods out of the lake bed, and piling up debris here as they brought in materials from the mainland to form their living spaces, establishing themselves in this borough near Tenochtitlan.

From the very top of the hill I can see the ceremonial and administrative center skyline of Mazatzintamalco. And using my mind's eye, it is possible to see beyond that a faint line leading out of Tenochtitlan. It is the Tlacopan causeway. Although they are too far away to be seen, there are many people coming into and going out of the great metropolis. I look down and see my friend Ahuiliztli (I call him Iztli for short). He's out of breath. He goes straight for the ground next to me and drops, exhausted, trying to catch his breath. I laugh at him. I always beat him to the top no matter how tired I may be. He's a little on the heavy side. He's carrying a sack strapped over his shoulder. I ask,

"What's that?"

"A new invention," he says, still breathing heavily.

"Let me see."

He sits up and brings the sack around to his lap. He opens a gap wide enough to fit his hand through and pulls out a finely polished obsidian stone. On the surface is a stick figure and other lines etched onto it. He says,

"Sit here. Watch this."

I sit beside him with my eyes fixed on the stone in his hands. He positions it to the sunlight and moves it slowly from left to right and back again. As he does that, I can see the stick figure become animated. The other lines I had noticed on the rock are actually the same figure but drawn in a different position. In all, there are about ten sketches closely etched onto the face of the stone. When the light hits in a certain angle I can clearly see the standing figure. Then as he moves the stone the light hits the second figure which shows an arm and a leg raised as if taking a step. This is how the illusion works. With light and drawings suddenly you have a sketch in motion. Iztli is always creating new toys or tools. He knows how to paint and mold things with mud. He even knows how to make houseware like bowls, vases, and other things but he doesn't particularly enjoy making those. He mostly likes to create things that no one else has seen before. I immediately want that rock. I ask him for it. He says he can't give it to me unless I give him something equally unique and rare.

Some days pass. I am home. It's a typical day. Nothing out of the ordinary. We are getting ready to have dinner. Suddenly a knock at the entrance. My nantli mother goes to see who it is. I can tell it is someone unexpected because mother shouts in surprise and joy. My tajtli father looks toward the door and a forced smile appears on his face. Then I look. It's Uncle Ohtli, my mother's older brother. The first and only pochtecatl in the family. My favorite uncle. I run to greet him ecstatically. I think he's happy to see me, too. He gives me a big smile as I hug him. Father is peering at me underhandedly. I have always suspected that he resents me being so fond of my uncle Ohtli, especially because I have been known to say that I want to grow up to be a pochtecatl just like him.

We sit down to eat. I sit next to Uncle Ohtli unable to turn my attention to my food which is getting cold as I am transfixed listening to him tell of his latest adventures. I can see all the sights, smell all the scents, and hear all the sounds in his stories. Not only is he a successful pochtecatl, he is an accomplished story teller. Mother does her best to get me to eat my food as she notices me ignoring it, but she is gentle so I ignore her, too. But then my father speaks up. Just one word firmly intoned: "TONALI". He has spoken my name. He needs not say anything else. It is a clear warning. I immediately straighten up and turn my attention to my plate as I try my best to listen to Uncle Ohtli. He goes off into some grown-up business with father.

They get into a back and forth conversation. I think Uncle Ohtli is trying to persuade him into some deal but father is the most hard-headed, least adventurous person I know. He is content with being a simple chinampa farmer by day and fire starter and overseer by night. An ostensibly prestigious position for an otherwise common man. You would think that the lighting of the night is within reach of any person with sufficient skills to make fire—and it is—but our custom is to place that duty on one man so that every night we reenact our gods' act of breathing life into the world, in essence igniting the fires of life or lighting up the darkness of the world. On the face of it, yes, it is quite an honor to hold that position. But on the greater scheme of things, in my opinion, it's a dead end. Once you are awarded that honor it is nearly impossible to relinquish your duty so, you are essentially beholden to the community to fulfill the task for life.

Father has been doing those two things since I began having a memory to recall. He will be doing them until the day he dies. He wants me to follow in his footsteps and learn about plants and chinampas. I haven't the slightest interest, although at the moment I have no choice but to work with him and pretend that I do enjoy myself at times. I don't. I tune out of their conversation and focus on my food. Suddenly, their conversation dies down and Uncle Ohtli turns to me lowering his voice and pulling out something which he had close to him all along but I had not seen. It is a small leather pouch.

"Who's ready for a surprise?" he asks raising his eyebrows. "You didn't think I came to visit empty handed, did you?"

I smile so big my cheeks hurt. He places the leather on my hands. I can't stop smiling. Father says unenthusiastically,

"What do you say, Tonali?"

"Thank you, Uncle Ohtli," I say.

"Well, aren't you going to see what's in there? Or did you think that the pouch itself was the prize?" Uncle Ohtli says this teasingly and winks at me as I look up with my frozen smile still stuck to my face. I open the pouch and turn it upside down. Out slides a little clay dog painted dark grey. For feet it has wheels at the end of its legs. It is a toy Xoloitzcuintli dog on wheels. Uncle Ohtli snatches it out of my hand saying,

"Take a look. It rolls smoothly!"

He takes to the floor behind us and pushes the wheeled toy across the room. I rise to my feet, run to it and kneel. Then I look at Uncle Ohtli as if to tell him to get ready to receive the toy as I wheel it back. We remain on the floor for some moments longer, tossing the toy back and forth. Each time we keep adding a little more distance between us and casting the toy as fast as possible to test the limits of this invention. As he tosses it back to me once more I suddenly have a realization which brings all play to a halt.

"Send it back, boy. Let's see if you can manage to steer it straight through these gates," he tells me as he sets up goal posts at the other end using his cactli shoes.

"Uncle Ohtli. If we could put wheels on animals like deer or jaguars, couldn't we use them to ride them and go places faster?" I ask genuinely curious.

"Well, I'm sure a jaguar would never let us mount it without chewing off our noses," he says as he comes closer and pinches my nose with his hand as if to pull it off my face.

"And as for deer, I've never known of anybody successfully riding one, although they are known to grow pretty big. But besides, I don't think we could attach wheels to their legs. That only works with toys because you push them with your hands. But maybe we could invent vehicles with wheels which we could then use by loading them up with things and push or pull them to our destinations. You know, instead of having to carry all these things on our backs? Imagine how much more we could move from one place to another?"

"Yeah, but at what cost?" my father interjects. "It is a man's pride to be able to carry and transport more than his weight in goods. Isn't that what you pochtecatl are commended for?"

"Well, yes, but what if we could double or triple our load by using a wheeled vehicle? Imagine the riches."

"But, again, at what cost? We are men. We show our worth by the strength and capabilities of our bodies like all creatures of the world."

"Except that we aren't like the rest of the creatures of the world. You said it yourself, we are men. We are not beasts. Animals have no choice because they don't have minds and hands, and language!"

"Yeah, but we were made strong for a reason. That is how you show your prowess, by the weight you can carry and the distance you can carry it."

Uncle Ohtli seems to ponder the thought, then says,

"Not exactly. What about all those canoes? You work in the chinampas. You've used a canoe on occasion when you need to transport waste away from the area, or to bring in soil, or rocks, or wood. Does that diminish you as a man? I don't think it does."

"Yeah, well, that's not the same thing. Using wheeled vehicles is for delicate men. What's next? Getting your woman to do the heavy lifting for you?"

That's always father's best response to a losing argument. Whenever he feels intellectually outmatched in a debate against someone, especially someone like Uncle Ohtli, he immediately resorts to low blows and petty remarks. Uncle Ohtli simply smiles and brushes it off. Their conversation etches into my brain because it is more than just an amusing match of perspectives. It is my inner self's voices; my inner duality debating back and forth. Who will be my role model? Who do I look up to as the mentor that I want to emulate? It feels somewhat disloyal in a way but the answer is clear, especially after this night. Underneath it all, I really do love my father despite having absolutely nothing in common with him. But I very much want to be like my uncle Ohtli when I grow up.

Sweet dreams...

It's the day after my uncle's short-lived visit. He has gone on to the pochtecatl headquarters in Tenochtitlan, and from there on to the great marketplace of Tlatelolco. He's told me many stories of those places. I can only dream of going to see them one day.

I meet my friend Iztli back at the top of Little Chapultepec. I've asked him to bring the carved obsidian stone with him. I have a proposition for a deal. He meets me there. We both have sacks with our respective items. I know what he has in his. He has no clue what I have in mine.

"So? What's in the sack?" he asks eagerly.

"I got a deal for you. What I have here is what you asked for in exchange for that magic rock you have. But with one condition."
"How can there be any conditions? I don't even know what you have there. Maybe I won't even want to exchange it for my magic rock."

"Believe me. You will definitely want to have this. It is unique and it is something that nobody else has around here. Besides, you can always make another magic rock."

"Not exactly. Obsidian stone doesn't grow on trees, you know. You have to get it straight out of the mouth of Popocatepetl. It's risky business."

"Shut up. You've never even been close to Popocatepetl! However you got it, I'm sure you can get it again. So, are you interested yes or no?"

"Hmm, well...okay."

"Okay, but like I said, there is one condition."

"Fine, what is it?"

"You will get to keep the original item in this sack but you will have to make me an exact replica of it. It was a gift from my uncle Ohtli from his travels to the Totonacapan lands. It has to look exactly the same. I don't want him to think that I didn't like it."

"Oh yeah? Well then out with it. Let's see what you have!"

I pull out the wheeled Xoloitzcuintli toy and put it up to his face to show it off to him. To my great disappointment he didn't even flinch.

"Is that all you have? That was your big surprise? There's nothing special about that. I can make one of those with my eyes closed!"

"Oh yeah? Well why haven't you made one then?"

"Because I didn't want to."

"Shut up. You've never even seen one of these things in your life!"

"I don't need to. I can make it in my sleep."

"Okay, mahuiztictlacatl 'great man'! Then you'll have no problem making me an exact replica. So, do we have a deal?"

"Hmm, I don't know. I mean it's not as unique and special as my magic rock."

Fuming inside I reply, "Yeah, you know what? You're right. Never mind. I guess I'll go back home and just keep this little useless toy to myself."

I'm walking away, putting my toy back into the sack, and having a hard time concealing my anger. If he doesn't attempt to bargain I'll just keep walking and maybe I'll get over the anger in time. But I have not gotten far and I hear him call out to me.

"Alright, alright. Gimme your damned little wheeled dog. It's a deal."

I turn to him with a sly smile and say, "See, I knew you would break. You're weak my friend. Weak!" I tease. Deep down I actually was counting on my hunch that, being such a curious investigator of novelty as he is, he would not likely be able to refuse my offer.

"Whatever. I just didn't want to see you walk home with your head down crying like a little baby."

"You want to see a baby? Here's your baby right here! Kiss it, girly boy!" I say this as I tug at my dangling boy parts, twisting and contorting my body in a strange dance, making faces at my friend as he stands there holding out his hand to receive the Xoloitzcuintli toy, simultaneously looking away and telling me to stop it.

Awakening...

Upon opening my eyes I was confused for a moment. Something about the place I was in was familiar to me but it seemed inappropriate for me to be there. I say inappropriate only because I somehow knew that this was a place I had left a long time ago and it was no longer a place where I would be waking from sleep. It took me a while to adjust my view. The sense of smell was the first thing that was fully functioning. The aroma of a childhood dish filled the room. It was the fish stew my mom would always make when we were feeling sick. A silhouette moved in front of me. I still could not tell things apart but only through their general outlines and odors. As for the figure walking about in my proximity, her smell was that of maize which she handled daily to make the tlaxkalli tortillas every evening for sale in the market as well as for our home use.

"How do you feel, Ali?" I confirmed my mother's voice as she referred to me by my childhood nickname.

"Nantli? What are you doing here?"

"Well, I live here. I still haven't severed

my vows to your father...in spite of everything."

I managed to have good enough sight restored to notice her devilish smile while she winked at me as she joked about leaving my father. It started to dawn on me that I had been partly dreaming and partly remembering segments of my childhood from the comfort of my parents home. The place where I had grown up. I suppose being at my parent's house facilitated that voyage into the past however unconsciously it may have been.

"What am I doing home? How did I get here?"

"That is the interesting part. You were brought by none other than a full escort of porters of the very own Huey Tlatoani Ahuitzotl. When I saw them standing outside our door I nearly fainted. I thought they were coming to take us all prisoner for some reason. You never see those people out here unless there is something or someone causing them problems they need to deal with."

As she spoke, I began to recall scenes from a very recent past, which explained how it was that I had ended up where I was and in the condition I found myself in. Tlatoani Ahuitzotl himself had thrust me into the gladiator ring in Tenochtitlan to fight for my life, and I had nearly failed, barely surviving the ordeal. My mother continued,

"They thought you were going to die. So they brought you here so I could say my last goodbyes, I suppose."

"What about my house in the city? Why didn't they just take me there. I have servants. They could have taken care of me."

"You had servants, darling. Past tense. And by that measure, you had a house. The pochtecatl officials took all your possessions as punishment for your betrayal. At least that's what the porters told me when they brought you here. The Tlatoani was quite generous, though. He sent provisions for your care. They haven't been back since then."

I realized that very moment that all my wealth, my possessions, my home, everything that I had worked so hard to attain had been stolen from me without a care in the world by those same fat, useless bureaucrats at the top. The very people who's coffers I had been stuffing with riches by excelling beyond expectation all those years. I suppose after thinking about it I understood why they would choose to do away with me in spite of my skills. I had gone over their fat heads and tried to leave them out of the "cut" by going straight to the Tlatoani himself. Had I struck a deal with the him I would have instantly gone from mid-level pochtecatl to possibly replacing one or all of those old windbags who headed the organization. Indeed I was seen as a threat. So what better way to ensure their survival than to eliminate the threat by robbing me blind and cutting me out of the trade? That was the worst part of the realization of my new situation. Once you were ousted by the top level pochtecatl, you were no longer sanctioned by the organization to engage in trade and commerce of that nature. The disheartening prospect of having to start again from scratch in life doing something other than the only thing I was good at must have begun to show on my face, I suppose, because mother placed her hand cupping my chin and said,

"Don't worry. Everything is going to be alright, Ali. Material possessions are not the true measure of a man's worth. Besides, you're young. You'll be able to make all of that up. The one thing to be absolutely grateful for is that you are alive. That is all that matters. And that the Tlatoani was compassionate enough to send you here so I could take care of you. Only the gods know what would have become of you if he hadn't rescued you when he did."

I saw her warm smile and thought I should keep some things to myself at least for the moment so as to not ruin her positive thinking. If only she knew that the Tlatoani himself was responsible for the condition I was in, she would have marched herself all the way over to Tenochtitlan, straight up to that bully on the throne and given him a real piece of her mind and a good scolding. Yes, I would just keep that information to myself...for now.

I laid back down, took a deep breath, and felt myself drifting off again into dreams of my childhood.

••••

(4)

Dream on...

At thirteen years old now I'm old enough
to begin wearing a loincloth. We are becoming
men, Iztli and I. Though, we don't see each other
much these days. Most of the time I am spending
it with father in the chinampa plots. Building
some, planting, harvesting. Taking others down.
Decommissioning them for a few months when
they have been exhausted, which happens very
infrequently. Most of them require just one
instance of decommissioning and then they are
good for another few years. It depends on the
location, what is planted on them, and how many
harvests they produce. That's what father says. I
try to motivate myself to adopt his worldview and
simply take what is there for me. What he is
providing. It is a good living. It provides security
and stability. But I cannot. I just don't understand
how he can be so content with such a simple,
uneventful existence year in, year out.

I'm standing on the edge of a chinampa
thinking about the way my life is shaping up.
Thinking about ways in which to force myself to
conform. Maybe I'm just a dumb kid full of
fantasies and dreams beyond his grasp. Maybe I

just need to grow up a little more and life will straighten me up; wise me up. Then I'll learn to be happy with what I have. Eventually marry. Build my home. Have children of my own. And raise them to do the same trade and not be young and restless...and stupid.

I've come to a grinding halt in my work, completely lost in thought when a voice jolts me out of my trance. I turn. It's a young man on a canoe passing by the chinampa. Momentarily, I am unable to recognize him or the man rowing the canoe. But then I get a clear fix on his face. It's Iztli. He's all grown up. He's only one year older than me but appears even older, more mature. He's got a noticeable, thin layer of hair over his upper lip. He looks like a Tenochca prince.

"Greetings, my friend!" he says.

"Greetings. It's been a long time."

"Indeed. It has been way too long for old friends to meet."

"You're doing well for yourself. Congratulations. I see you have the means to commission the labor of a designated transporter. Where to, old friend?" We are overly formal with each other, because it has been some time since we have been friendly and it just feels like we are strangers again.

"Your praise is much appreciated, Ali. But

I am not a wealthy man yet. So I am not able to commission this good man's service. I am, however, being summoned by the administrators of the great Calmecac school of our capital city of Tenochtitlan. It is they who have sent for me in style!"

"Indeed?"

"Indeed, my friend. I have been awarded a full tuition and residency for me to continue my training in the fine arts. Who's to say, I may even be commissioned by the great lords of Tenochtitlan or by the Tlatoani's themselves one day to paint murals or sculpt statues of them, or any number of things. Hopefully, I will be allowed to use my own criteria and not be expected to replicate other artists' works."

"I hope that you are able to achieve all of your dreams, my friend. I shall ask the gods to guide you to the success that you deserve. We all know very well that you have all of the talent, imagination, and the skills to make a great name for yourself." I pause momentarily as he nods in gratitude. Then I continue with my praise.

"I shall be proud to call myself your friend and will tell my children about how I once was best friends with the great Ahuiliztli. An artist, inventor, and friend to the lords and Tlatoani's of the great city of Tenochtitlan!"

"Stop. You flatter me too much, dear friend..." He stops speaking briefly, looking at me

25

intently as he scans my face for a reaction, then says with a mischievous look and a big smile, "Ok, keep on with the flattery."

This is the first moment in the conversation that we break off into a familiar laughter. The kind of laughter that you can only share with your comrades, your friends, those sharing a space in this world with you at your same economic, social, spiritual level. It is both an ice-breaking, cheerful laughter, and a bone chilling, somber realization that our lives are veering off into opposite directions so vastly different, that to say that we will see each other again or we will get together in the future to catch up is just words valid only in that instant and then they become irrelevant and false as soon as his canoe rows away.

I am beginning to feel a strange sensation of sadness bordering on tearfulness. His departure is the least likely culprit, for I suspect that it is the fact that I am remaining which stirs my emotions so terribly. I cannot face him anymore.

"Well, I must return to my work. I hope to see you sometime when you come to visit. Let me know so you can tell me about all your adventures. Safe trip and may the gods be with you, friend."

I'm turning away, trying to widen the space between us so that my watery eyes become blurred from a distance and hopefully he won't notice that I am vulnerable.

"I'll be doing my apprenticeship with a renown Mexica artist. In fact, he is the one who recommended me to the Calmecac after seeing my works. Perhaps you could find a master under whom you could apprentice in Tenochtitlan and we can share in the adventure!"

I turn back to look at him and smile. I wave a goodbye and nod as if to say that I will do that. But we both know there is no chance of me getting out to the big city on an apprenticeship. Farm boys don't get to be apprentices to renown Mexica lords. They receive all their training from their fathers and the Telpochcalli; that is the school for everything farming and other low-level trades, and military training. A school for commoners mainly.

I can see from the corner of my eye that after a short while he finally motions the rower to proceed and off they go in the direction of the city in the center of the world, Tenochtitlan. I keep walking, acting as if I am searching for something on the ground. Liquid is beginning to completely blind me as it engulfs my eyes forcing my lids to blink and let the torrent break free of my constraints and my face becomes the source of two mini-waterfalls. I kneel as if to pull some weeds. But it is all to mask my pain. How I wish this very moment for some giant, or the gods themselves, to come pull me out of this place like a weed and plant me elsewhere where I can flourish like a flower in all its colorful splendor.

5

Mothers' nightmare...

A year has passed. No one has heard from Iztli since he left to the Calmecac in Tenochtitlan. Not even his parents know what has become of him. His mother worries. It's all she talks about to the other women in the neighborhood and at the market and at every chance. They are starting to avoid running into her. My mother is sympathetic to her. She's even invited her to the house on a few occasions. She lets her talk her heart out and tries to console her when she inevitably cries, which is always. I'm inclined to believe that Iztli is just too busy having the time of his life. What would be the point of leaving this place if all you wanted to do afterwards was to keep coming back or sending word of your comings and goings? It doesn't make sense. I'm sure Iztli has too much going on for him over there to concern himself with this place. And as for his parents, I'm sure he plans to come visit soon. But mothers worry. I suppose that is somewhat of a curse. No matter how old their boys grow they always see them as their babies.

I can tell mother is being influenced by Iztli's mom. It's obvious in how she looks at me sometimes. How she tries to spoil me by giving me my way more than usual and preparing me my favorite meals on days Iztli's mom has visited. She even stands up for me a lot more when father scolds me for whatever reason. I do somewhat like the treatment but at the same time I feel it inappropriate. After all, I am almost a fully grown man now. If I were anybody else I would be mining the situation for all it's worth. But I find myself strangely more repelled by it than not. So I am spending more time alone, away from everybody whenever I can...

6

Dream away...

Atop Little Chapultepec a tree has grown to near maturity since that time when I struck a deal with Iztli for his obsidian rock. I'm not sure where I have left that thing nowadays. I'm sure it's somewhere in my room. But up here I am at peace. It is the only place I find where I can escape and go see the world...in my mind, at least. Uncle Ohtli gave me a great gift last year. It is a replica of a book from the Maya lands. This serves as a great vehicle to let my imagination wander far and wide over the lakes, beyond the mountains, down into the lowlands, and deep into the jungles to be among the Maya peoples. I have trouble understanding what is written on those pages. But I still open it when I'm up on the hill by myself. I imagine that I can read and make up a story to go along with the symbols. In no time, I have an entire story written by me (in my head) to go along with the symbols of the book, so that if anyone were to ask me to read to them I would read them this book and no one would know the difference, because no one in these parts knows the first thing about reading.

In the Telpochcalli they teach us to read

only what is necessary. And only to those who show some kind of ability or natural inclination to writing and reading. I'm one of the few. But the training is actually based around farming concepts. Again, not at all something I can immerse myself completely into. So it serves me no purpose when trying to read anything else, especially something written in a foreign language like the book Uncle Ohtli gave me. Still, I am proud of myself in my mastery of the local teachings. But I feel that I am not seen as the brightest or most endowed with ability because I simply don't apply myself. I can't. When the pond is so small that only the little fish have room to swim, the big fish simply go belly up. It's not a lack of motivation or will on their part. It's a lack of space for their fins to actually work as they are supposed to. I'm the fish going belly up. I'm suffocating in this little pond. But I do have breaks once in a while. Like this week. Uncle Ohtli is due to arrive tomorrow on his way to Tenochtitlan from his travels...

It's getting dark and I'm still sitting under the tree. The beauty of this spot on top of Little Chapultepec is that no one else seems to care that it is here. None of the other youth or adults seem to even realize that they, too, could be taking their retreats up here, away from the drudge of everyday commoners' lives. Perhaps it is because they all are content and comfortable that way. As long as I am alive I hope no one ever tries to come up here to meditate in my spot. Although I miss Iztli and our times up here, I still enjoy returning every chance I get. It's my spot. Always will be.

I see the bonfire being set in the now fading outlines of my neighborhood below. It is my father who is lighting the fires of the night. Soon he will be spreading torches all along the streets, placing them on carefully prepared receptacles on outside walls so that the entire neighborhood will be lit up and people can walk about as in daylight. I'm tempted to go down and ask to help carry the fires to their different locations. But he has never invited me to assist him in that. I think it is out of some feeling of disappointment in the fact that I do not relish his farming teachings. He is very passive aggressive like that. So to communicate that I am unworthy as a man to share in the lighting of the night, he excludes me by not inviting me. Serves me well. I think it keeps me hungry for something different. Something he could never give me. And when I achieve that, whatever it may be, he will have to deal with his own feelings of inadequacy for having been unable to create a world which could spark some sort of wonder in me, his only son. If only I had a clue as to what I could do to strike out on my own and create that something new and different?

··

(7)

Dream ticket...

It's the following day. Uncle Ohtli arrives early in the morning. He must have traveled all night long by canoe from the mainland, and therefore, must have slept all along the way. He looks fully awake, fully animated. I am so glad to see him that I don't even bother to mind my father's jealous, underhanded looks this time. It's like I don't even care anymore if he knows outright that I would love to follow in the footsteps of Uncle Ohtli and not his.

Mother prepares some food. We all eat and Uncle Ohtli tells us he must go to the local market to deliver some announcements on behalf of the traders and merchants from the great marketplace of Tlatelolco, where he is headed. I beg my parents to let me accompany him to the local market to hear him speak to the crowds. My father ignores my plea, but that was almost expected. I look straight at mother who has always enjoyed a fairly equal say to my father when it comes to family or household dealings, unlike most women in our neighborhood who follow their husbands' lead at all times.

Mother looks over at my father who stubbornly refuses to acknowledge that anything has been asked, so she turns to me and smiles, nodding...

We are moving through the crowd in the market of Mazatzintamalco. I've been here before with mother but mainly on the outskirts of the marketplace outside of the major hustle and bustle. This is for two reasons. One, her product is limited and in high demand, so she sells them fast. Two, she prefers to stay outside of the main market square because of her fear of losing me in the crowd or getting lost herself. She comes here to sell bundles of tlaxcalli. Father comes here as well, to buy resin and wood for the fires and torches for the lighting of the night, but he's never invited me along...and I've never asked to come with him. But being here with Uncle Ohtli makes this day one of the most impactful of my young life.

Although Uncle Ohtli is clearly taller than me and both my parents, something about this day and the location we are in has made him appear to me as a giant among dwarfs. I feel as if I am looking up a lot more today. Looking up at him but also looking up at the enormous public buildings and massive teocali pyramids that seem to reach the clouds as we make our way further and deeper into the market square. I'm almost tempted to grab his hand because by now I am literally bouncing back and forth from one person to another as the crowds have become as dense as the prickles on a prickly pear, and as mindless and scattered as startled birds in flight. Although I am growing, I am no match against the fully grown merchants, farmers, warriors, jewelry makers, food shop attendants, tortilla sellers, livestock, patrons, and other people who are moving and dashing to and fro. For the first time in my life I feel truly small, insignificant, and out of my league...and I like the rush.

Uncle Ohtli leads me to a small clearing where a man has gathered people around him and he is reciting something to them. Uncle Ohtli reaches close to the man's ear as if to tell him a secret or ask him for a favor. I cannot hear what they say to each other, for the crowd is loud and animated. The man raises his hands over his own head as if to alert the crowd that he will speak now. He says a few words to the restless crowd and then my uncle Ohtli takes the center of the human circle. He sounds powerful. His gestures and his voice make him appear like what I would imagine a Mexica lord would sound addressing large crowds from the top of the Huey Teocalli great pyramid of Tenochtitlan. Suddenly, the crowd begins to heckle my uncle for some reason and he attempts to reassure them. As I push through closer to my uncle, I am able to hear him better.

"This will not interfere with your product demand. You will not be forced to lower the price of your goods. We are not competition. Far from it. We would be bringing goods and materials which are only found outside of the center of the world. From far off places. But we need to petition your calpulli local government of Mazatzintamalco to establish our very own station here in this market. If you sign the petition you will automatically belong to our union which would protect you and your business from unfair market manipulations and other problems faced by independent merchants. It's a win-win situation if you think about it. All we need is your inked handprint on this scroll and your name symbol next to it. You will all receive an official certificate indicating your membership and protection under our union after we have all the signatures and obtained the authorization from the city calpulli."

The crowd is looking much more amenable. My uncle's charm, presence, and skill in oratory prove to be too much for the masses to resist. After discussing some specifics among each other the crowd begins to form a line to sign my uncle's petition. Seeing this, it reaffirms what I had already concluded long ago: this is exactly what I want to do when I am a fully grown man. I want to be a pochtecatl like my uncle Ohtli. I want to address the crowds in big city market places. I want to influence people to support my cause. I want to charm the crowds to do my bidding. And I especially want to travel to places beyond the navel of the world in the Valley of Mexico-Tenochtitlan.

On our walk back to my neighborhood I tell my uncle what I have decided I want to do with my life. He smiles at me as if I have surprised him with my declaration but deep down I know he knows my heart's desire.

"Perhaps one day you may get your break, young Ali. You are a bright young man. Full of wit, and clever. Sharp as an obsidian blade!"

I smile broadly, my chest swollen with pride.

···
(8)

In my wildest dreams...

It's early morning. The sun has yet to be born on the horizon. I am woken by a heated discussion coming from the other side of the wall. It is father and Uncle Ohtli in a verbal back and forth. I cannot hear her, but I am certain my mother is there as well.

"Look, Amoxtli. I know you don't think highly of my profession. Frankly, I don't think highly of yours. But we respect each other. We both know how to carve a path in our lives by our own wits and with our own hands. Although with me it's more of a symbolic use of hands because I mostly use my words. But that is the extent of the difference. We are men engaged in valid professions. I know that you would like nothing better than to pass on your profession to your only son. All men want that. But is it possible that maybe Ali isn't cut out for what you do? Wouldn't you want to support him if there is something he wishes to accomplish even if it involves going into a different livelihood than yours?"

"He is my son and he will do as I say. My father was a farmer. His father was a farmer. And

I am a farmer because of their teachings. So will Ali make a fine farmer. He doesn't need to go off dreaming and fantasizing about adventures and thrills. He'll end up a beggar in the big city. Here he has security."

"I'm saying just think about it. Look I will leave you this form here. It has the insignia of the pochtecatl department administering the program for youths. Ali is a very bright, capable young man. I have seen people half as intelligent as he make a very good living for themselves. He would make a fortune in this business!"

"This isn't about being a rich man. There is more to life than material riches. I want him to grow up to be a moral man with great virtues. A man with riches on the inside. My decision is final. Take your form with you. He will have no use for it!"

"Dear Amoxtli, certainly we can discuss this with our son and see what he wants. After all, he is becoming a man. Shouldn't he be consulted on matters regarding his path in this life?" My mother says, interjecting on my behalf. I am happy to hear her do so, because I was beginning to feel a sense of panic at the thought that my entire life is being decided for me at this very moment and the one thing that could offer some promise of a change in direction—the form— could be taken away if my father had his way.

"But Chimalli, I know what is best for our

son. He will be a man like his father and his grandfather. Working with his hands will be the best life for him, especially since you and I know that he is a dreamer. If we don't intervene he could end up throwing away his life chasing fantasies."

"Surely you mean that he knows what is best for himself, beloved Amoxtli. And, yes I do agree that his father and grandfather are great, strong men. That is why I fell in love with you. Because you are a provider and a protector. But as a father to your son you should also be like the steps on a ladder for him to rise above and support him if he sees something that inspires him to devote his life to."

Mother pauses for a moment. Surely there are some non-verbal communications taking place. I can see it in my head. My father with his stubborn look that can only be softened by my mother's charms. Mother rubbing his arm, giving him a sideways glance. Who knows what that could mean. I dare not imagine. Perhaps mother bribing him with a promise to grant him something that only she can give him; communicating as only lovers can.

"At the very least," mother continued after a few long seconds, "let us keep the form. I'll put it away and we won't think about it for a few days. Then, when you feel the time is right, we will sit down with Ali and we will discuss his future. It is the only way, my love. Otherwise, if you impose your vision of his own future he will resent you for the rest of his life. I know you don't want that. I don't want that either."

"I can do just fine having an ungrateful son. It doesn't hurt me whatsoever. He would only be hurting himself."

"I know you could handle that, my love. But you know that I could not bear to see the both of you hating each other. If you will do it for no one else, do it for me." I can hear him as he releases an exasperated and loud exhalation, finally giving in to my mother's pleading.

"Fine," father says dryly. Deep down I know it is an act. A way to save face. He was sold on the idea of at least keeping the damn form since the moment mother intervened with her full charm in play. Father can be very stubborn and intimidating to many, but when it comes to my mother's touch, he turns to atolli cornmeal.

"If you were to let him explore this possibility I would personally make myself responsible for him in the capital, brother Amoxtli," Uncle Ohtli states enthusiastically, having noticed a softening of my father by my mother's interventions.

He continues saying, "I will be going to the market in Tlatelolco and staying there for a few weeks. Thereafter, I will be at my apartment in Tenochtitlan. He could be my apprentice. I have many contacts whom I could introduce him to. I'd make sure he starts on the right track. And he is a fast learner, so you can be sure he will rise quickly in the business."

Uncle Ohtli sounds animated as he is moving about, gathering his belongings by now. I hear them shuffle around and begin to say their farewells. Uncle Ohtli is heading out the door. I am tempted to come running out of my room to give him a great, big hug and thank him for offering a glimmer of hope in my life. But I know that if I do that they will know that I was listening in to their entire conversation and that would only serve to make father double down on his rejection of the idea. I stay in my room and thank my uncle in my mind, smiling brightly as the rays of the sun begin to shower my face through the window overlooking the dawning sky outside.

....

(9)

Love's young dream...

We are out on the chinampas. Father is heading a crew of workers building a new plot. I lead a crew of boys weeding out another chinampa. Every chance I get I am celebrating the developments of the early morning. Father has not noticed, or has chosen to act as if he doesn't notice but I have had a smile on my face the entire time. I am eager to obey his slightest requests. I'm doing everything in a cheerful and energetic manner today. In spite of the hard physical aspect of the work, the day goes by fast.

It's early evening now. I'm grabbing my Maya codex and am about to head out the door on my way to Little Chapultepec. Father stops me before I can exit.

"Ali. Perhaps you can help me light the fires of the night? That is if you are not too busy."

I am baffled. The entire day father has not been his usual self. Usually he's always demanding things and ordering me around. Today he has let me make my own calls out on the fields. He's asked me what I think about the logistics regarding the new chinampa. As if I know better or at least equally as he about the construction of those floating fields. And now this? Asking me if I want to join him lighting the fires of the night? This is strange. But of course I say yes.

He allows me to assist in igniting the fire. I have always thought it was easy. I suppose it is because whenever he does it, it looks like such an effortless task. I take the stick and the piece of wood. I begin to rub vigorously. I am doing it wrong. Father intervenes only to offer tips. He does not scold me for doing it wrong. He does not push me aside to do it himself. He simply advises and steps back. I begin to gather a good rhythm. Soon I start to see a plume of smoke rising. It takes me so long. I am sweating. The night is upon us. If it were father doing this first step, we'd have the fire going by now and the torches already up at the different locations.

People are beginning to gather around us. They are wondering why they are still in darkness. Where is the fire? Soon it is dark black all around but only for a few tiny embers. I can no longer see the plume of smoke. I think I have botched the whole thing. Father steps in. Maybe he is going to finally shove me aside and take over. No. He simply unloads a handful of dry grass around the rubbing wood pieces. A few moments later the sparks of new fire begin to emerge from the darkness.

"Now lightly blow on the arca," says

father gently as if to not spook the fire away.

I blow onto the tiny fire embers on the grass. They begin to multiply as I keep blowing until flames emerge. Father throws some more grass on top of the flames and they become seemingly enraged, rising up and licking the air.

"Grab any little sticks and bark and put it all in the middle stacked together," says father. I follow his instructions diligently.

We finally add the big logs of wood. This fire in the center of our neighborhood serves as the light for the nightly communal gatherings of friends, old people drinking pulque and telling stories of the past, young men and girls promenading around the fire full of giggles and bravado. Father and I begin to light the rag-tipped stakes dipped in the resin mixture he prepared to aid in the slow burning. We have some assistants helping distribute some of the torches. It's a couple of boys a few years younger than me.

Finally, we are down to four torches. I take a couple of them and head off in the opposite direction as father to set them in place. On my last post I come across Iztli's home. Someone is standing by the doorway. It is Moyolehuani, Iztli's young sister. I suppose it has been too long since I have come by their home, for I do not recognize her. She has grown significantly. I am struck by her beauty. It is like I am meeting her for the very first time, even though I used to tease her just as much as her older brother did.

Huani (how we've always called her) is smiling at me. She is holding her family's torch stick which she is to use to gather fire from the lit torch I post near her home. She comes close up, smiles again looking deep into my eyes, then lights her torch and takes that fire into their home. I manage to see the fire illuminating their chimney and some candles and suddenly I see the faces looking back. It is her mother and a small toddler. Perhaps a younger sibling I have not met being that it's been so long since I have come by their house. I turn away and begin to walk back toward the bonfire. Before I can get too far Huani returns to the doorway and calls out to me.

"Hello, Ali."

I turn in a snap upon hearing her say my name. Her voice is a novelty to me. It is no longer that of a little brat girl giggling and bothering us then complaining when we give her a hard time. This voice is music. Not angels singing but Xochiquetzal incarnate.

"Greetings, Huani," I say looking for words to prolong our interaction. "It's been a long time."

"Yes."

"Have you had word of your brother? He is a fine artist and a capable young man."

She giggles. I am nervous.

"Why so formal, Ali? I didn't know you were such a bore. At least that's not how I remember you."

She's teasing me. The little Huani of yesteryear I could handle easily. Tease her back. Mock her crooked front tooth. Make fun of her furry braids. Laugh at her for coming in last in a race while she cries. But this Huani...this grown, shapely, beautiful Huani is another creature altogether. I find myself wanting to lick her crooked tooth. I want to entangle myself in those loosely crafted braids. I want to let her win any and all races if only she'll let me win her touch.

"Forgive me...I mean, sorry. It's just been such a long time since I last saw you. You look so different. I feel like I hardly know you. I didn't know if I should be polite and well-spoken as is the custom among strangers."

"Strangers? Is that how you see me?"

"Well no. Of course not. I just meant..."

"It's okay, Ali. I understand. Maybe we could get to know each other again like we used to. But this time don't pull my braids...at least not too hard."

She cracks a devious little smile and my loincloth begins to feel tighter on me as my body responds to her charms faster than my intellectual brain can process what is happening. She steps out of the doorway and we begin walking toward

47

the bonfire in the center of the neighborhood. We are both seemingly swept up by some sort of magical hypnotism that prevents us from realizing that we are still just kids and, at any length, we are unspoken for.

People have made themselves comfortable by now in the common grounds. Some playing instruments, making music. Some singing. Some dancing. The old folks are laughing hysterically in their alcohol-induced reverie. My father sees me approaching and for the first time I see him smile at me as if he were proud of me for some reason. I don't understand it but this day has turned out to be one of the most gratifying in my young life.

(10)

Reawakening...

I awoke in the middle of the night. For a moment I thought I had just dozed off after hearing father and Uncle Ohtli's discussion about my future. But I noticed that the room felt different. I asked myself, where did the sunlight go? Did I fall back to sleep all day long into the night? Then I realized that not only did the room feel different, I felt different, too. Every part of my body felt longer, and thicker...and everything hurt. I was back from the past. I wondered at the oddness of having dreams that simply reviewed my past experiences. Never had I experienced such dreams before. Then again, I had never been at a point of near death. It dawned on me that that was exactly the cause for this revisiting of the past, because I had been courting death and so my entire life had been flashing before my eyes every time I returned to sleep. I felt too weak to get up, so I tried to shift around in bed. Mother must have been employing some powerful remedies on me. How she did it to feed me was a complete mystery, but I suppose she got it done somehow. To think that only a few weeks before I was on top of the world. A fully independent, self-sufficient man. A man of possessions and position in the world...to some extent. And then to end up at my parent's home, in the care of my mother who had to change my sheets and wash off the refuse like when I was a completely dependent child. Just thinking about it made me wince. I felt myself slipping back into a deep sleep. The room was so dark and silent and the medicine so strong that I couldn't fight the slumber even if I wanted to. Truthfully, though, I didn't really want to fight sleep. I wanted to go straight back to those times of discovery and ignorant optimism for what was to come. I rocked myself back to sleep hearing the rhythm of my breathing and feeling the thumping of my beating heart.

(11)

Wet dreams...

I'm back under the tree on Little Chapultepec. It's early evening. Father has already started the communal fire for the lighting of the night. I suspect he may have been looking for me, because he's been inviting me to assist with that ritual every night since the first time he asked me five days ago. But tonight is different. I could not make myself available for that because there is something much more important and exciting than the lighting of the night: Huani. She was heavily scolded and severely punished that night we went for a walk among the promenading youths around the communal bonfire. Her father was enraged to have his only daughter seen out and about with a boy as if they had both been spoken for by each other's parents. After a few days passed we agreed to meet under the tree. Tonight is the night we agreed upon.

I'm nervous. For the first time I will be alone with her; or for that matter, with any girl. I don't know what exactly it is that a man and a woman do together when they meet out of sight of others, but I have a strong indication from my body as to what will be involved in our exchange.

My boy part feels so engorged and stiff, throbbing and pulsating with anticipation for the unknown that it almost hurts in a most deliciously new way of experiencing pain. I have to press down on it to soothe it. And also to hide it away. Although it is getting dark, I'm sure that Huani could tell there is something out of shape down between my legs.

I see a silhouette. I'm sure it's her. As I said before, nobody else comes up here. She's wearing a simple, white huipil that reaches down past her knees. Her hair is loose. She looks like she is ready to go to sleep. She sits down next to me. The smell of flowers in bloom engulfs me as she comes closer to hug me in greetings. I'm clueless as to what to say, so I say nothing. I'm glad we have sat down. This allows me to cover my out of shape loincloth with my cloak and just focus on looking into her eyes.

This night the moonlight is so bright that although the sun has died on the horizon I can still see Huani's face clearly. Her hair is cast to one side over her shoulder and blowing gently in the air. The moonlight bouncing off her eyes makes her head seem like a lantern lighting my path to her lips but I hesitate. Do I touch her? I ask myself. Do I obey my mouth that begs for me to lick her lips and plunge my tongue into hers in search of that crooked tooth and her warm, moist tongue as well? I think too much. She brings her face to mine and our lips brush each other gently. Inexperienced, ignorant lips don't know what to say or what to do the first time the chemistry of love ignites on their surfaces. But I feel a shockwave of energy travel through my face down into my body, through to every pore and every limb and digit. A warm wetness covers my part as it begins to throb once more demanding touch of some sort, in some way. My entire body feels the most powerful urge to close the gap between us and let skin meet skin, allowing our movements to guide my entry into her being; to fill the gaps between her arms, between her legs and possibly within her heart in a way which only I was meant to fill this very night.

We wrap ourselves in each other's arms and simultaneously begin to strip our clothes until we are completely bare. She looks down, reaches with her hands and instinctively rubs my already volatile erection. I tremble. I lay her down and spread her legs. I poke around like the novice that I am, desperately searching for my place within her embrace. I don't know where or how but I know that somehow I must penetrate her or I will die. She takes a hold of me with her hand again and guides me as she raises her hips to receive me. I am poking and pushing upon her searching for the path that beckons me, exploring her terrain until we reach the gates of her heaven and I begin to slip magically into another universe. The warmth inside her hips is comparable to nothing I have ever felt. Her lips between her legs are even more mysterious and exquisite that I feel my body convulsing with waves of electricity shooting straight through my spine. I want to devour her completely. It is a need more than desire become one with her. In a very literal sense I don't trust the gods and I don't trust the universe and much less anyone living to respect this mad love, this uncontrollable fervor, this terrible need to merge with her and freeze time in the moment of ultimate ejaculate, at the pinnacle of orgasm; that outer layer of existence where ecstasy resides among the heavens in the hands of a conceited deity. Feeling myself levitating by now, I begin my release bursting like bubbles at the foot of a waterfall. Then erupting inside her with the mad intensity of Popocatepetl, shattering all thoughts and outside sensory input. Uncontrollably convulsing, then shrinking into her arms as I am rendered utterly vulnerable and limp.

And then we are still. Only our lungs pulling air desperately as we gaze in wonder into each other's eyes. Heart beats thumping in our ears. Our bodies sliding over each other on the sweat that has pooled between our bellies.

I slowly slide out and slip off her to lay face up with my arm still clinging onto her. I feel the gentle grass blades as they buffer me from the ground. Huani curls up beside me, riding my hip as she raises her leg over me, resting the knee on my spent, flaccid, and wet member. Her fingers run circles over my chest as we gaze into the starry sky feeling the warm breeze drying the sweat off our bodies.

"I miss him," she says. I know instantly who she is referring to.

"I miss him too," I echo.

"I simply cannot bear the thought of something bad happening to him."

"Don't worry. I'm sure he's fine. He's very talented. He's probably been kept so busy he doesn't even have time or energy to send word. But I'm sure he'll come visit sometime."

"What if you're wrong? What if something bad happened and he needs help? Or worse, what if we never see him again?"

"Don't say that, Huani. You worry too much. My uncle Ohtli says that the capital is so enormous and full of things to do and places to see that you could spend your entire life living there and never get to see the whole city. That is how big it is. Think about it. Iztli was always destined for great things. He's just very busy, beyond what we in our simple lives out in these places can conceive of."

"There must be something I can do. I need to know what has become of him."

"What would you do? You're only 14 years old."

She looks at me as though I have hurt her.

"I'm sorry, Huani. I'm just saying that there is very little you can do, being that you have no means, no family in the capital, and you are just barely coming into womanhood. Who's going to take someone like that seriously in the big city? In fact, they'd quickly take advantage of you. My uncle Ohtli has told me what happens in the capital to orphans found in the streets. They are either put to do hard work, or they disappear, or they are put in those houses to be used by older men."

"Used? How?"

"I can't imagine. But what do you think an older stranger would do to a helpless girl like you? I don't want to even think about it. I would kill a man who tried to put his hands on you."

"You would?"

"Yes. I would," I say looking intently into her eyes, sensing that a unique moment between us has been reached. "I will never let anyone hurt you. Even though it's like we have barely met each other, there is no doubt in my mind about my feelings for you. I love you, Huani."

I look into her eyes as I say this. The entirety of what constitutes a heart and soul within me reaches out to her through my words as my eyes observe her reaction expectantly. She looks at me with a strange aura of mystery and wonder as if she were trying to decipher something beyond human comprehension. I anticipate hearing her replicate those words that have fallen from my mouth; waiting for her tell me she loves me, too. But in place of those words only a smile appears on her face as she slides her hand across my cheek in a soft caress; a gesture that strangely feels like something mother would do when she is filled with tenderness for her baby boy. It is love...just not the love that a man seeks from a lover.

"Then take me to the capital, Ali. Help me find my brother. Please, I beg you."

"I can't do that," I reply trying to conceal my disillusionment. "Better stated, WE can't do that. We don't have the means nor any idea what to do even if we were to get to the capital."

"You said it yourself. You're uncle Ohtli lives there. We could look him up and ask if we can stay with him for a while. He's your family. I'm sure he'll say yes. Then after some time when we have gotten situated we move into our own place together. Imagine it, Ali. You could come home from a long day's work everyday, and I could be waiting for you to serve you as my man."

She moves her leg off me, reaches down with her soft, smooth hand and begins to lightly feel the shape of my member. First with her fingertips then slowly bringing her palm and cupping me and maneuvering about until gradually I begin to feel my part swelling up, rising again, and soon it's throbbing and wet in her hand as she whispers to me in my ear. My hands begin to caress her, exploring her every curve and crevice. My tongue and lips savoring hers. My love grows. My hunger for her increasing with every whimper of her delicate sexual arousal. Huani climbs on me opening her legs, impaling herself on my erection. A soft whimper escapes her momentarily as I tear again through her virginal veil. We make love once more locking eyes with eyes, matching moan to moan as the moon shines her blue light on us enshrining our silhouettes onto the top of that little man-made hill like footprints upon sand. Markers in time that even when they are eroded by the coming and going of the tide, will always remain in spirit as testimony of a moment shared which nothing can undo.

(12)

Rude awakening...

"Ali...Ali, wake up, son. It's time for your meal."

Back to the present again. I was awakened by mother. She had a bowl of wuehxolotl turkey stew with squash.

"I was dreaming again."

"Again? Who did you dream of this time?"

"Huani."

"Oh, yes, the famous Huani. Or should I say...infamous?" she winked at me.

"It was the night when we decided to leave for the capital. Remember?"

"How could I forget. That's when your father pretty much disowned you. He was so angry and upset with you. And I was, too. Leaving like that without telling us anything? You caused me many sleepless nights until we got word from your uncle Ohtli that he was watching over you. I begged him to send you back but he told me you had made it very clear you would not return. I thought, well at least he's with my brother and I know he will take care of him. But that was still no reason to overlook what you had done. Even years later when you apologized to us, I still held some of that resentment for what I felt was a lack of compassion on your part—for me especially. I'm your mother!"

"Forgive me, nantli. I never meant to hurt you. Either one of you. Tajtli never let me explain even if I tried. I've never gotten to ask him for forgiveness in person. Has he ever said anything to you about it?"

"You know your father. He was a deep well of secrets. Nothing ever got out. He refused to talk about it. I pleaded with him to go bring you back home from the capital. But he refused, saying that you were no longer his responsibility. That you had made your choice and would have to face the challenges of life on your own. He didn't even approve of your uncle Ohtli helping you out. But don't worry, conetl. He missed you. He really did. Your father was tough and demanding, but he had a great heart and a great capacity to love. And he did love you since the moment we both laid eyes on you. He was there at the very moment of your birth, you know?"

"I love him too. Very much. It's just that he never made it easy for us to talk about anything. Much less to say I love you."

"But that doesn't mean that he didn't, Ali."

"I know, nantli. I know. But sometimes people just need to hear the words said."

"Oh, I know a lot about that, dear. Your tajtli thought that because he had told me once that he loved me he never had to say it again. To him it felt as if it cheapened the power and meaning of the first instance. He'd say that only liars repeat things over and over to convince others that it is truth, but in reality it's all lies. I suppose he was right about that. But that was your father."

"You think I could talk to him now? You think he might be willing to come in here? I haven't seen him at all since I got here. Come to think of it, I wouldn't be able to tell even if he had been in this room. Sometimes I feel like I have been out of my body, floating in around in empty space, though I still rise to eat and talk with you while my energy holds up. It's strange...Can you call him in here?"

"Baby, I wish I could. I would give my life just to see him in this house one more time. But you very well know that your father has been gone for years now."

"Gone? Where to?"

"To the highest level of Mictlan heaven, I'm certain."

My mother's words were as plainly stated as they were cutting in the deep recesses of my heart. I felt the sharp pain of realization. The realization that indeed my father had gone into the afterlife years ago, and I had been aware of that occurrence, yet at that very moment, reliving the past in my dreams, and enjoying the conversation in the warm and caring company of mother, I had forgotten the fact. In a way it was as if I were losing my father again to death. The finality of it was what had driven me mad with thoughts of regret when I first heard he was gone years ago, because I knew that I would never have a chance to show him that I would be a success and, perhaps because of this, he might have left this world feeling like he had failed me.

Yet it was because of my father's presence in my life that I had grown to be the confident and strong-minded man that I became. But when he died I was still in the process of becoming that man. So I had not gone back home in triumph. And I had not had the chance to talk to him and apologize for all the little gestures of ingratitude on my part as I was growing up. I never meant to offend him or dishonor him. And yet it all was too little too late when he passed to the next life. At that moment as I lay on my own death bed, as it seemed, I felt the sorrow of loss and meditated on the memories of my father as mother fed me the soup in silence until I finished eating and slipped back into sleep. Luckily for me, I once again found myself traveling back to the past in dreams, the only place where I was finding consolation and reprieve from the pain on my body and now, too, the pain in my heart.

(13)

Pipe dream...

It's late. The fires of the night have extinguished or have been put out along with the communal bonfire. All is darkness. We know that her family is out and about in search of Huani, so we wait them out as much as possible. Only the gods know what will happen when she arrives home. I'm inclined to believe that her father will literally end her young life. Especially because she has been seen with me in public and tonight we both went missing. Father is waiting for me outside our home as I approach. I can sense that he is in a sour mood, though I cannot clearly make out his facial expression. But it must be one of disapproval.

"Where were you?" he interrogates in a stern tone.

"I was out in Little Chapultepec."

"It's late. You must obviously be aware of it."

"I am. I fell asleep over there. Didn't realize how late it was until I woke up a little while ago."

"Truly?"

"Yes. Truly."

"And Huani? Did she fall asleep with you, too?" His remarks feel like an insufferable mockery. Being called out in this way catches me off guard and I feel instantly slighted, but at the same time embarrassed for thinking I can pass something past father. After all, he may be simple-minded but he isn't stupid.

"I was alone," I reply barely managing to sound convincing, although I'm sure he is not buying it.

"Well, she went missing at around the same time that you were gone. Could that just be a coincidence?"

"I guess."

"You guess? Everybody knows you two were together the other day. I saw you with her, too. Are you going to give a full accounting of you and your chosen partner like a man does? Or are you going to go inside and hide behind your mother's huipil?"

I can say nothing. My chest is beginning to expand and collapse forcefully as I feel the blood rush to my face and my lips firmly clasping together at the insult hurled at me by my father. Of course I was not going to go hide behind my mother's huipil!

"Yes. She was with me. I love her." My voice trembles as I finally confess.

"Ah. Well then. That changes everything. I am proud of you for acting like a man and being truthful. But that is not all that one must do as a man when he loves a woman. If you love her you must show it with actions. Words mean nothing if your actions contradict you. Taking your woman away from her family when you have not put forth your face to speak about your love is not something men do. Penetrating a woman with your member and using her body to satisfy yourself does not make you a man. It makes you a boy concerned merely with seeking pleasure and satisfying his own urges without thinking of what comes from that union."

"I didn't...We didn't..." My attempts to counter his accusation are feeble. Perhaps it is because he speaks the truth of what I have done.

"You didn't what? You didn't come together as lovers? You realize that that does not matter anymore, don't you? You took her into hiding, away from the eyes of others. Whether you came together or not is irrelevant. Everyone from now on will believe that you did. Do you understand how that could affect a young girl? She could be labeled for life as a loose woman. No one will respect her. No man will want to marry her."

My manly efforts to be strong and brave in

front of my father are starting to crumble. Tears are falling from my eyes. I don't know what hurts more: that I have been caught in an outright lie or that no matter what I do I cannot stop myself from crying. Father puts a hand on my shoulder.

"There's no reason to feel shame if your heart is in the right place. And I do believe that you love that girl. That is why I have spoken to Huani's father already and we will all be meeting tomorrow to discuss you and Huani's future. You will marry. It's the only way to save her honor and reputation. And, since you have been showing much improvement at work, I am prepared to collect the necessary means and make you a loan for you to build your own home. I will help, of course. And I will assign you half my crew so you can start your own chinampa operation. You will start by building your own plot, then go off and get your own work orders. Again, with my help, of course."

Father is smiling at me by now. My tears have ceased in part because of the fact that father is not giving me a serious scolding anymore but more so because of what he just said. Again the talk about my future is coming from people other than me. I realize that my father never intended to consider Uncle Ohtli's offer. He never even intended to sit down with me and show me the form Uncle Ohtli left behind so that we could discuss together, respecting me as the growing, maturing man that I am becoming.

"Well?" he continued. "What is your response? Is that not good news? You won't have to go hiding away anymore like a scared boy. Everyone will look at you and say that is a man!"

All I could muster was a meek "Yes."

"Yes?"

"Yes..."

"Very well, then it is done. Go to your room. We have a long day ahead of us tomorrow."

I walk into the house in shock. Mother is standing close by. She has heard the entire conversation. I barely notice her there in the darkness but I imagine that there is a soft, tragic smile on her face. She knows very well that father hasn't been quite honest with me as to the options in regards to my future. But, although she is usually effective in swaying his determinations, this time there is a girl involved and she believes that father is correct in stepping in to make the arrangements for our wedding. So she says nothing.

I am in my room. I know what I must do. This is goodbye. I wait for them to go to sleep. With the moonlight flooding my room I am able to gather some clothes and my Maya book. Luckily I am able to locate the magic stone that I had traded with Iztli years ago along with the replica of my Xoloitzcuintli toy on wheels. There is only one thing missing for my departure: Uncle Ohtli's form. I creep into the cooking area and remove a small, clay idol that guards a secret compartment on the wall. That is where mother places things of value such as jewelry, currency...and the form. I take it and put the idol back along with everything else, hoping they won't notice for many days that I have had access to it.

Upon returning to my room, moving about as silently as possible, I put everything in a sack which I tie over my shoulder and across my chest. Midway climbing out the window I pause and look back into my room imagining myself walking again throughout our home just to feel it vibrating one last time before I go. I also picture myself hugging mother firmly and receiving a kiss on my forehead from her lips as she had always done until I asked her to stop some time ago because it made me uncomfortable. Then I see myself coming up to father, standing straight, chest to chest, face to face, and like a man taking my father's hand and forearm into mine and shaking, saying, "Thank you, father. I shall make you proud upon my return." And he responding, "Go with Tlaloc, my son. May he rain torrents of good fortune upon you!"

I climb out of the window and walk away from my childhood forever.

(14)

The fog of sleep and death...

Something pulled my sheet at the foot of my bed hard enough to wake me. It was night time again. I knew I was back home in the care of mother because in my dream I had just climbed out through the window where a shower of moonlight highlighted the window frame. But upon waking at that particular moment, all I could see was darkness. Only the breeze coming through informed me that indeed there was a window there. I shifted around on my side ready to go back to my dream where I could find some level of joy, when from the darkness in my room I heard:

"Even in dreams you're still that little boy stuck on chasing fantasies, huh?" A dry, hoarse voice said, seemingly unconcerned with the possibility of waking up my mother in the adjacent room.

"Tajtli? Is that you?" I could not believe what I was hearing. The likelihood that I was confused and that there was a stranger in my room instead of father crossed my mind, but why would he be talking in a conversational, and chastising tone...exactly like father?

"Still debating in your head? Pull that big head of yours out of your ass, boy. It is me. And I am here to kick your ass straight back out of this deathbed!"

Even though by now I was convinced it was my father's voice, I still could not believe how much more belligerent and frank he was being with me at that moment. It was as if we had grown older together and there was a familiarity among the two that carried off into outright crude and unfiltered language, which was not common to my past experiences with father. To be honest, it was actually kind of fun and seemed much more metropolitan of him, even though in life he had detested the big city and its ways.

"What are you doing here, tajtli? I thought you had gone to the ninth level of Mictlan long ago."

"Yeah, well. I'm here now. Life is good in Mictlan, but seeing as you can't get your shit together I am forced to take a break from paradise and come knock some damned sense into you!"

"I don't need your help, father. I never have before and I still don't. Besides, a spirit man can't help me," I responded dismissingly as I lay back down to rest my head.

"Careful how you talk to your father, you son of a—!" He held his tongue and cleared his throat. Then he proceeded more thoughtfully,

"Well, I won't finish that phrase out of respect for your mother. But you watch your tone with me, boy. Spirit or no spirit, I will kick your teeth out."

"Look, if you don't mind, tajtli, I would rather go back to sleep, ok? I'm in recovery here."

"You're done recovering, boy! That's what I'm here to tell you. Any more recovering and you're going to end up meeting me in Chicunamictlan where I came from!"

"What do you mean? I don't feel fully recovered. I'm still in pain. I sleep almost all day every day. I hardly know when mother is in here feeding me or changing my sheets. You call that being fully healed?"

"I call that your mother being your mother. She does her best but she is no expert when it comes to those drugs she is giving you. You do know they were sent here by the Tlatoani himself, don't you? If I were you I'd question his motives."

"But mother never said they had sent medicine, too. She just said supplies. I imagined food and other things like that."

"Well, there are drugs in you alright. She's thinking it's good for you. That is what the Tlatoani's own physician told her. Nobody is going to question a royal medicine man."

"I thought I was on my way to actual healing. I've been dreaming a lot about good things from my past. No nightmares or anything."

"Yeah, that's what happens when you first start going through the levels of Mictlan. But by the time you realize it you are neck-deep in a torrential river which you will only be able to cross if you had a Xoloitzcuintli dog in life and actually treated it right. Only then would that Xolo be willing to help you out across the river. And I'm not talking about your wheeled toy. I mean an actual dog to care for. And the river is just the beginning." He turns his eyes to the floor and begins pacing in a small circle back and forth, all the while holding up a hand throwing up fingers as he lists the different ordeals the recently deceased go through to get to heaven.

"Then you are confronted by a windstorm of flying knives slicing you up, then walking through cold deserts, then wild animals chasing you trying to eat out your heart, and an alligator wanting to swallow you whole. Yeah, kid. It's quite a series of ordeals. But well worth it if you make it through. I made it, so I'm good. But you, you're not ready to go. Not yet. So you need to get your ass off that bed and claim your balls again, boy. Stitch those ahuacatl fruits to your midsection and get back out there and start living again!"

"You mean right now? It's the middle of the night. Can't I wait until the morning to try to get up from this bed?"

"Oh okay, you big baby. What else? You want me to go fetch your mommy to come rock you back to sleep?"

"What is with you?! You were never this annoying in life. Does everybody become obnoxious when they enter into Mictlan as spirits?"

"I wouldn't know. I've never been there," he said, folding his arms as he shrugged his shoulders.

"What do you mean, tajtli? You just said you came back from Mictlan to wake me the hell up and get me off that medication."

"Yeah, that is true, about the medication. But as for being your father coming back from the dead, nope. Not a chance. By Xolotl, you still believe in fairytales?! What a moron."

"Hey, what the hell?! If you're not my father, then who in crap's name are you?!"

"I'm a figment of your imagination, you fool. You are hallucinating! It's the drugs, man. The drugs! See? That's what I mean. You got to get off this junk and get back to living or you're going to die in here. And if you die, don't say I didn't warn you."

I hadn't quite noticed but as the conversation progressed, father had begun transforming into different versions of himself mixed with aspects of other people that I had met in my many travels. He changed so much that he began to look more like a formless mass of clay and then like smoke, and finally the smoke began to clear, and I could hear nothing but silence again. The interaction had roused me enough to make me rise up on my elbows again like when I was being fed soup by mother. I called out to him again but he was gone. I laid back down and thought long and hard about what had just taken place until a big smile broke out on my face and I felt myself slipping back into dreams, smiling and thinking of my trash-talking spirit father who had just paid me a visit.

≡

(15)

Broken dreams...

I'm walking down the pathways of my past under the moonlight. This night has seemed eternal. First the discovery of love on the summit of Little Chapultepec, then the face-off with father. And now here I am, the only soul awake walking past my neighbors' houses on my way to an uncertain destiny. I decide to walk by Huani's home. If only to look at the house and imagine her beautiful body and her lips smiling at me once more, for I don't necessarily have the intention to try to take her with me. But as I come near the house I hear sobbing.

I approach quietly, trying to stay within the shade of the houses to avoid detection. The sobbing intensifies as I narrow the distance between me and a low-set window of Huani's house. Creeping up slowly against the exterior, I sneak a peak in the off chance I might be able to make out Huani's silhouette in the moonlit night as I did earlier atop the hill. I see her. She is sitting up on her bed and crying. I let out a soft whisper but she doesn't hear me. On the ground beside me I am able to locate a small pebble which I take in my hand and cast it in toward her. It lands on her gown. She looks up at the window and is startled at first. The instinct to flee and sound off an alarm is evident on her reaction but something stops her. Undoubtedly, it is that she, too, remembers what my silhouette looks like in the night so, she comes closer until she's next to me at the window.

"Ali, what are you doing here?"

"I wanted to see you once again. What happened? Why were you crying?"

"You won't believe what my father is going to make me do. He told me he's found me a husband and he's going to marry me off to him. I don't even know who it is."

"He didn't say who?"

"No."

"If you had a choice who would it be?"

"I don't know. I don't think I'm ready for that life. Eventually maybe. But not now."

"What if I was the groom? Would you want to marry me?"

"You? Well, I don't know. It's just too much to think about right now. Why do you ask?"

"Because father told me the same thing tonight. He said he had made arrangements for me and that we would be meeting with the girl's parents tomorrow."

"He did? Who did he make arrangements with?" Huani's tears suddenly disappear as the look of amazement overcomes her face, causing her eyes to open wide, again taking in the moonlight and reflecting its blue rainbow at me to my delight.

"With your father."

She looks perplexed. Her eyes blink continuously as she tries to process what I have just said.

"Me? You are to marry me? So you are the one my father was talking about?"

"I suppose. Unless he made plans with others. But my father said he'd talked with your father."

"Why would they do that? I don't understand."

"Because of what we did tonight at Little Chapultepec."

"You told your father what we did?!"

"No. Of course not. But he figured it out.

They knew we were both missing and they put it together. So to save face they are going to play it off as if the intention had always been for us to get married. That way people won't talk bad about you. It's to protect your honor."

"Protect my honor? From what or from whom? I don't think I need someone to protect my honor. I just know I am not ready to marry. I'm sorry, Ali..."

She pauses momentarily to give me a look that I detest coming from her. It's a look almost of pity, if you can actually feel that for someone you love...or at least someone you have been sexually intimate with. This is not how I want to end this night of my greatest discovery to date. It seems she is completely oblivious as to how her demeanor affects me. She is likely more caught up in her own self-interest regarding this forced marriage arrangement thrown at us. I try to look unphased by her ill-thought blurtings as she continues:

"But I guess none of that matters now. If they make it official tomorrow, that is what we will have to do."

"You don't need to apologize to me. I'm not ready to marry either. At least not here. I'm not ready to start the rest of my life in the swamps of Mazatzintamalco as a chinampa farmer. I'm leaving, Huani. I'm going to the capital."

"What? When?! Tonight?"

"Yes. I have decided to go look for my uncle."

"Oh, Ali. Will you take me with you then?"

"You meant it when you said you wanted to go?"

"Yes of course!"

"Shhh, lower your voice," I caution as her voice rises with the excitement of my news.

"Yes. I meant what I said. Please take me with you."

"Okay, then grab a few things and meet me around back. Be very careful not to wake anyone. And don't take too many things. Just enough for a couple of changes."

I walk around the back of her adobe home and wait hidden in shadows. Something on the back of my mind is scolding me, pointing an accusatory finger, judging me. Why have I accepted to bring Huani with me? It is clear she is not in love with me, isn't it? Or maybe she does love me but it takes time for a woman to become completely immersed in the sea of love in which a man (or in my case, a boy) immerses himself seemingly instantaneously. Part of me knows that this voice on the back of my head is my moral upbringing instilled by my father, therefore I can almost hear his voice reflected. But another part of me is quite clearly my own conscience telling me what I know deep down to be true. Huani is fond of me, loves me for being someone she has connected with on an intimate level and shared the beautiful act of lovemaking. But she is not *in love* with me. And as for my motives to bring her along...could it be that I am simply thinking of my own pleasure, just as father had admonished me for earlier? Am I just being a selfish boy concerned with his own gratification and maybe deep down I don't truly love her as I have convinced myself that I do?

A shuffling of feet among the shadows snaps me back-to as I sense her approaching and we sneak out of our neighborhood for good. We walk all night following the path to the central market place that I had walked with Uncle Ohtli. She's hanging onto me as if she were teetering on the edge of a cliff, afraid to fall into an abyss, in spite of the fact that the moonlight accompanies us all the way and allows us to have a clear view of our surroundings.

We come closer to the island center and can see some public buildings and temples with still-burning fires in braziers lighting the overnight temple-keepers on duty. We walk stealthily making certain to stay along the shadows of the city center, for although no one knows us, the fact that we are so young can raise alerts as to our purpose there and someone might decide to detain us until they find where we belong.

There is also the danger of meeting a worse fate before reaching the capital, so I make sure to avoid interacting with anyone until we get to the lakeside docking, where men are loading goods onto a canoe destined for Tenochtitlan in the wee hours of the morning. I negotiate with one man to take us with him in exchange for the sack of coffee beans from my parent's savings, the Maya codex, and the magic stone which I demonstrate to him how to use in the light of a flaming wood pile. This impresses him very much and he agrees to take us as soon as he is loaded up and ready.

It is midmorning when we reach Tenochtitlan. With directions from several people we walk endlessly, it seems, until we come to the pochtecatl central office where I present the form Uncle Ohtli had left for me. I ask to be directed to his apartment in the city. They are able to give me his address and we finally make it there by early evening. Luckily he is home. We have a wonderful time the first days after we arrive. Uncle Ohtli is very accommodating and generous. He takes us on sightseeing tours of the city. We even make it to a ball game in the great city square. It's a major event. Things are going well. I have enrolled in the Young Pochtecatl program Uncle Ohtli had told my parents about. I like it very much. It mostly requires me attending classes to learn the principles of the trade. All of this is on a stipend which I will have to repay once I begin my actual work as pochtecatl.

Nonetheless, the training is long and rigorous. It involves learning to read, write, count, perform arithmetic, public speaking, appraisal of goods, sales tactics, and negotiations training. It takes me away from Huani pretty much all day every day. I get to see her only in the evenings. But I think it is worth it because as soon as I get started earning a living, I will move us to an apartment of our own as we had discussed and then we will officially start clean together. This is the plan, at least until the moment I come home early one particular day. I am excited because I have been told that I will be leaving on my first trip the following day with a group of trainees. This sudden trip has been causing me some anxiety all day in the knowledge that I will be gone for some time and Huani will not be able to come with me. What will she do while I am gone?

When I reach the apartment, I go straight to our room where I expect to find Huani waiting eagerly to receive me like most nights. As I enter the doorway I see a couple laying in our bed. They are clearly entangled in the act of love. I realize it is the back of Uncle Ohtli's head that I am staring at. Momentarily, I imagine that, this being his house, it could very well be Uncle Ohtli and a woman he has brought home. But this consideration is quickly debunked as I hear a series of familiar female moans of intimacy and pleasure. It is Huani whom my uncle is penetrating in our own bed. The chill of shock and betrayal freezes me until I am unable to verbalize anything or move at all. Even blinking ceases. I am paralyzed. Uncle Ohtli suddenly turns and sees me there. Huani jumps up and shouts in surprise as she attempts to cover herself up. A single tear teeters on the edge of my eyelid, gathering volume until it is pushed off by its own weight, running downward accross my face, then falling freely until it splatters on the floor.

"Ali. It's not what you think, son," says Uncle Ohtli, struggling to his feet as he covers himself with his cloak.

Suddenly my body unfreezes and I turn my back to them. I walk out. They are following me trying to explain that it has all just been a mistake. I start running. There is a storm brewing and thunder is masking my uncle's pleas to come back and let him explain himself. It's fitting because I do not care to hear him out. I get lost in the city, hiding from the rain and from the attendants of a lesser god's small temple where I sleep that night.

I don't know if it is an internal sense of guilt and fear knowing that I am in a sacred space without permission, or perhaps it is the movement of people in the temple as they hum and chant through the night invoking the deity— or perhaps it is the god himself sending spirits to disrupt my sleep—but I am tormented through the night with a vision of death and destruction. In this dream vision I see fires in the distance glowing and lighting up the clouds into bright yellow and orange orbs. The sounds of agony echoing throughout the city tell of unspeakable horrors at the hands of marauding invaders. These visions keep waking me startled and wide-eyed, peering into darkness. I can hardly sleep on this night.

(16)

Living Nightmare

Once again I awoke not from the dreams of horrible death in that temple, but from the memories of my past that I was reliving in my convalescence. There must have been tears streaming from my eyes as I relived past traumas in my sleep, because as I opened them all I could see was a blur. However, it was clearly early morning. I could tell that much because the gentle light of daybreak illuminated my window, although it scantily lit up my room. A figure entered my quarters lighting her way with a small torch. "Mom," I thought to myself at first. Then I spoke the word as I tried to clear my eyes to make her out better.

"Pardon me, my Lord?"

"Lord?" I thought. This woman was not my mother. I began to clear my vision. Suddenly I could see a familiar face, though not mother nor any family, but one of my servants from my home in Tenochtitlan. And then it dawned on me that I wasn't even in my childhood home anymore but in some palatial complex very much like those found in the city.

"What am I doing here? How did I get

here?" I demanded answers from my servant.

"You were brought here by the royal guard, my Lord."

"Nonsense! I was at home in the care of my mother just last night. How did I end up here? What is the meaning of this? Did you feed me the mushrooms so that I would lose my presence of mind and then smuggled me here?"

"No, my Lord. You have been here many days now. I was brought here only several days ago. They said it might be well for you to see a familiar face when you came back from your inner voyage."

"Inner voyage? I had no inner voyage. I was at my childhood home. I was recovering well. Being cared for by my dear mother. It was real. I did not dream that."

"I'm afraid you did, my Lord. But I am here to serve you well as always. I will see to it that your recovery is swift and as pleasant as possible."

"No. I will send for my mother instead. If I was indeed dreaming, then it must have been a sign. Something was trying to tell me to go to her...or bring her to me. That is what I shall do."

I noticed the look on her face as I said these words. It was the look of pity and nervous sorrow. Nervous because she knew that I did not like bad news and somehow I knew instantly by the look in her eyes that that was precisely what was waiting to fall off her lips.

"What is it? What happened to her?"

"Forgive me, my Lord. I must tell you terrible things about your beloved mother. She is of this realm no more. By decree of the Reveared Speaker Huey Tlatoani Ahuitzotl your mother, along with your entire village, were executed by troops of the royal guard."

"WHAT!? The entire village?"

"Yes, my Lord. The entire village was burned to the ground. Nothing was left standing. And all other remaining members of your family living anywhere in the city and its surroundings were sentenced to the same fate."

"Everyone? Even Uncle Ohtli?"

"Well, they say that he remains a fugitive. But they are hunting him down as we speak. Sooner or later they will catch him. They always catch them."

"But if exterminate us is what they want, then why am I still here? And you?"

"I do not know, my Lord. I ask myself the same question. Why was I spared when all the rest of your servants met the same end as your... family."

I got up from the bed numb by now. A slow ringing sound was building up in my ears, and although my servant kept speaking I could no longer hear her words. I gave her an empty glance as I passed by her on my way toward the window. She must have realized that I was lost in my sorrow now and, therefore, nothing she said reached me anymore. Her lips stopped and closed as her glance slowly turned downward leaving me to my grief.

My feet were in full command of my body, though I felt myself stiff and cold like a corpse as I somnambulistically moved across the room. For a moment I was an empty vessel. Heartless, for there was no beating in my chest. Lungs empty of oxygen feeling myself drowning in despair, unable to breath. When I reached the window the sun shone his fire on my face but I felt no warmth. My eyes stared into the distance searching for my village, my childhood home, and at that moment I knew that the vision I had had in my youth as I slept in that temple, and that I had been dreaming of again only the previous night, had been a vision of my home ablaze; a premonition...nay, prophecy! That was why I had cried so much through the night. My spirit knew the truth of what would occur while I went roaming through the levels of Mictlan and back, even though I would not know until my rude awakening.

I peered through the window hoping and expecting to see some smoke still rising on the horizon as I searched for the memories of the place where I had grown up. Somehow the possibility of seeing a smoke trail seemed to offer some lifeline or some link indicating that my past had been real. That the people of my childhood and the spaces we had shared were worthy of protection and conservation not just by those directly involved and personally invested in them, but also by the greater self that is represented by a leadership, a government, a nation. But instead of that protection, my mother and all that I loved had been eradicated and burned like refuse into ashes and nonexistence.

I pleaded with the gods to send my mother to me floating safely upon a cloud, unharmed. But that would not happen. And so it was that for a moment of unbound delirium occasioned by that terrible news about the fate of my mother and all the people of my village, I had an out-of-body experience as I lost my self-awareness, only returning to it after I felt a light touch on my shoulder. It was only then that I realized that I had been shouting out a prolonged and gut-wrenching howl that had brought my servant to tears and compelled her to reach out and touch me in an attempt to offer me some comfort. But there was no comfort to be had. There were no thoughts of healing anymore for me. There was only one thing on my mind. The men who had done this had to die. The Tlatoani himself would not be spared. The whole city with its evil ways was beyond saving. At that moment I had resolved, once and for all, a stark determination: Tenochtitlan...must...fall!

The X Series

End of Book 1

MONSTER OF WAR

...As I entered the private chamber and the attendants retreated closing the massive doors behind me, I found myself beginning to feel quite nervous and unsure of myself. I had the sack of goods, which also held the written scrolls, carefully resting over my right shoulder. Since I was meeting the Tlatoani for the very first time, I had used a considerable amount of my personal wealth to purchase the most exquisite garments and adornments in the city so as to honor the Tlatoani's presence in style.

I walked cautiously. The place was dark and chilled. The silence in the chamber was impressive in comparison to the busy streets and pathways of the city outside. I felt as if we were many feet underground. The only light source was a dimming ray of sun cast into the chamber through a circular opening on the ceiling. It created a spotlight directly in front of a monolithic throne made of volcanic rock. To each side of it were single, large torches lighting up the Tlatoani's ceremonial chair. But I did not make out the figure of the Revered Speaker Ahuitzotl. For a moment I assumed that, as all royalty or people of importance, he would have me wait as long as he wanted until he decided to give me the time of day. So, I yielded my step just before entering the spotlight and decided I would simply wait, since there was no way I could leave now. Doing so would be an affront to the Tlatoani that could bring about potentially deadly consequences. I like to think that I was a daring and risk-taking young man, but one thing I have never been is suicidal. So, I simply stood there waiting to be seen, when from behind the throne came a dark, deep voice saying:

"Step into the light." It was the Huey Tlatoani himself.

At first, I knew the voice was coming from the direction of the throne, but I could not see anyone. Gradually I adjusted my eyes in that contrasting darkness with the light of the torches and the beam cast from the ceiling, and noticed a faint silhouette behind the backrest of that elevated seat. I took about three more steps and landed right in the middle of the natural yet fading spotlight. I simply looked ahead at the throne, since this new position further prevented me from seeing anything clearly but the torch fires, until I saw the figure move in front of one of the flames headed for the throne.

The torches magically magnified as the Tlatoani sat down and soon I could clearly see his full face and upper body positionedon that chair.

He appeared to me as a giant, big and robust. I could trace the silhouettes of his thick upper arms protruding from his wide chest. His eyes were piercing daggers that warned of an implacable inner rage and thirst for war and conflict. It was no surprise to me that it had been this man who had subjugated recently some of our fiercest enemies whom his predecessors had tried but failed to conquer. Some said that he defeated whole armies all on his own, shooting lightning bolts from his eyes and tearing out the enemy's hearts right where they stood with his bare hands. There was no uncertainty in his demeanor. He did not blink. He did not shift around in his seat. Not a single digit on his extremities twitched and perhaps even his own heart and lungs did not proceed in their rhythmic motions unless he allowed it. It was as if this one man commanded all life on earth without exception, and life itself obeyed him.

"You did not honor the traditional ways upon entering into the presence of your Tlatoani. Were you not instructed as to the procedure?"

"Forgive me, Revered Speaker. I may have unsuspectingly consented to forgo the instructions that your attendants were offering. I suppose I misinterpreted what they were asking me and I simply nodded, so they excused themselves. Please accept my apologies, sire. In my highly excited state I am just finding it hard to settle into a quiet disposition and be mindful of my surroundings. It is completely my fault."

"No need for apologies. I absolutely abhor the antiquated and stuffy ways of this dreaded office. I'm not one for pomp and diplomacy. My strengths and longings are derived from the art of war. The thrill of conquest. The very taste of the blood of my adversaries. These priests and cemitqui politicians want their precious capital to be some sanctimonious, god-worshiping, sissified city—they can have it!"

As the Tlatoani paused to look at my reaction, I struggled with the question of what to do or say in the tense and uncomfortable silence. He must have seen me squirming, for I am quite sure I noticed a slight smirk on his shadowy face as he sat there like an immovable statue carved onto the side of a mountain. It almost seemed as if I were simply hallucinating , hearing a non-existing voice coming from that solid figure that appeared to be joined to the gigantic throne as if they were one whole piece. He continued after what seemed like an eternal pause:

"I was promised a great score of goods and information. Is that sack over your shoulder containing my belongings?"

Nervously I said, "Yes, highness," and handed the sack over to him. Things were not exactly going as I had imagined they would. In my mind I had seen myself in complete control of the situation. From the moment I was introduced to the moment I opened the sack to show him the items I had brought specifically, for him. I had envisioned myself taking one item out at a time and telling him where I had acquired it and perhaps offering a short description of my struggles to attain them. This, I believed, would make the impression that I was very skillful in my acquisitions and that I carried the Tlatoani's interests on the front of my mind at all times. Of course, after hearing him inquire as to the items I had brought with me, I very much heard the thinly veiled directive in his question. I would later learn that his questions never really were simple questions nor requests but tacit commands for people to obey immediately. So, I did.

To my astonishment, the Tlatoani began to take one thing out at a time from the sack to analyze and quickly discard as if it were worthless trash. I was appalled. Some fine, holy Quetzal feather bundles tossed aside into the darkness. A newly crafted obsidian ceremonial dagger, equipped with a luxurious handle made of dried and hardened leather, adorned with the rarest jewels, carelessly thrown aside to a certain destruction on the solid rock floor tiles. Next, the never-before-seen and completely new item in our realm: the Spanish hand-held mirror on a shiny, metallic frame, also strewn across the room. I couldn't believe what I was seeing. But suddenly I noticed something. All the items, shatter-proof or not, made absolutely no sound as they flew off into the black space around us. I suppose the Tlatoani quickly intuited my pondering, for he simply said:

"You place too much value on outcomes, Pochtecatl Tonali. That is one of man's most basic flaws. And one that will undo you unless you stop deriving your self-worth from ordinary, earthly things. Worry not for these objects you have brought here. They will not break. My attendants would die before letting anything fall from my hands onto the floor. Even in war, they are the very first to dive straight into the fray not so much to kill the enemy as to ensure that neither my weapons, nor my body, ever visit the ground after a serious blow. That is what training and valor engrains: watchfulness. That is what this city—this empire—needs in our warriors and in our representatives. But this new 'religious awakening' brought on by my sycophantic, pious nephew Moctezuma is turning Tenochtitlan into a dim-witted realm full of pussyfooting flagellants whose only purpose in life is to burn incense and sit around talking about the end times and the second coming of Quetzalcoatl. A great pile of nonsense! He shames the great name of my father Moctezuma Iluhicamina!"

"I'm glad to know that, highness..." I mumbled.

"What?! You're glad to know this city is becoming the shame of the world?!"

"Oh, no, your highness! I—I meant I'm glad to know that you clearly have everything well thought out and have a contingency plan in place for everything you do. So, I'm glad those items you took out are not simply breaking, for some may be of great importance to you and your plans for our empire."

For an instant it seemed as though the Revered Speaker and I had found a common ground. This allowed me to break free of my fear-instilled paralytic disposition and start going face-to-face with the so-called madman of Anahuac. Nonetheless, I retained some degree of trepidation knowing that he could at once decide to have off with my head and that would be the end of me.

"What do you know of my plans for this empire, peasant!?" The Tlatoani's sudden turn to explosive interrogation promptly derailed my thought process.

"You think I don't know who you are? I keep very good information on all my subjects like an astronomer peering into the cosmos every night. I pay particular attention to those stars that seem to be moving in ways that they should not be moving. Usually it is those stars that truly make me wonder. They make me question their purpose, their...intent."

"Highness, I assure you I am here with your interest at the forefront of my agenda—"

"So, you admit you do have an agenda!"

"No! No, your highness. I did not mean to imply anything beyond my wish to put myself at your service. Please forgive me, your majesty. I am new to this. I'm not exactly trained on matters of debriefing and royal procedures."

"Finally, you make some sense in your fumbling around. So, the question is, Pochtecatl Tonali, why are YOU here? Why you, instead of your pochtecatl lords? It is they who deliver the news of import and bring the rare commodities and goods directly to me. Why has a nobody requested a part of my very busy day? There are procedures to follow, Pochtecatl Tonali. You continue to show that you are just not willing to abide by any rules, isn't that so?"

By now his direct challenge to my very presence in that chamber melted away my resolve and I was like a defrosted mountain peak laid bare of snow and ice, showing my true colors. It was a plain, stark fact that I was completely out of my league. At that very instant I realized that I had made a huge mistake in circumventing the process and sidestepping the pochtecatl lords. If I survived the wrath of the Tlatoani in this cold, dark auditorium, I would be lucky not to suffer a very public execution, or at the very least a severe lashing, at the hands of my pochtecatl superiors. Those men were not known for being kind and forgiving. As I said before, those who commanded at the helm of the pochtecatl business were as a royal family; a dynasty in their own right. A state within the state. With rules and guidelines for every single thing. Highly bureaucratic, highly efficient in getting their way...and highly lethal when faced with opposition to their designs. I knew that very moment that, either way, I was going to be maggot food very soon. Unless I found another escape. But how? I had nowhere to go. I thought this time, indeed, I was doomed.

To my unpleasant surprise, the Tlatoani suddenly broke out into a roaring laughter so calloused, so sinister that it both irritated and terrified me. But it brought me back from my inner dialogue in which I had gotten lost. The Tlatoani had seemingly tried to address me with some other question but noticed that I had apparently lost all of my inner fibers and just stood there like a porous board, hollowed and immobilized by terror. Looking in my eyes and at my general appearance, he noticed that, indeed, I was scared stiff. This just tickled him to no measure.

"Relax, lowly pochtecatl! You look like a toy Xoloitzcuintli that barks incessantly but when confronted, it simply lays down and plays dead!"

The insensitive crude continued laughing uncontrollably. I felt terribly offended and completely humiliated. But something told me that his demeanor was starting to change in a positive way. Perhaps he was relaxing a bit. That could prove to be a good thing for me. But I couldn't be sure. After all, there was a reason he was called the madman of Tenochtitlan. He was highly volatile and unpredictable.

"Is that what you are, lowly pochtecatl? A toy Itzcuintli?" The Tlatoani asked as his laughter seemingly evaporated from one instant to the next and all that remained was that steely, glaring look in his eyes.

He snapped his fingers in the air without removing his eyes from me. At that gesture a few more torches were lit around that enormous enclosure as the sunlight disappeared and I realized that I had been standing in complete darkness.

"Bring me Xolo Ahuitzotl," the Tlatoani

commanded to no one in particular.

I thought he must have been talking about one of his sons sharing his same name. It would have made perfect sense for a supreme ruler of the Mexica to have named one or several of his own offspring after himself. After all, this wasn't just any ruler, he was the great warrior-king Huey Tlatoani Ahuitzotl; possibly the greatest and fiercest of them all.

To my surprise, instead of seeing a younger version of the tyrant in front of me, I noticed the same attendant who'd stepped out return with a dog in tow. A Xoloitzcuintli. But not the funny looking playthings you would see in the great market for sale as companions for little children. This Xoloitzcuintli was a beast in true form. Tall, slender, clean, muscular, and entirely menacing. I didn't know what purpose the Tlatoani had in mind having his ferocious animal, already eyeballing me and growling, brought into the chamber. I trembled at the thought that this psychopath would be cruel enough to have me meet my end in the jaws of a vicious monster.

"This is a real Xoloitzcuintli. Not a toy Itzcuintli. You must wonder why I named him after me, don't you?"

"Yes, sire," my voice shook.

"I did so because this breed of dog is a fighter in true form. They never back down. No matter how overwhelming the odds. They could be facing a jaguar—two jaguars! They will fight to the death. I am just like this dog. I want to build a society of Xoloitzcuintli. Which one do you think you are? Like Xolo or like an Itzcuintli toy?"

"I...ahh, I am your humble servant, majesty," I muttered feebly.

"Ha! Spoken like a true lap dog! Very well, then. From this day forth you shall be known as *Pochtecatl* Itzcuintli. Do you reject your new name?"

"Highness, I don't believe that I have been given proper opportunities to prove my worth as more than a mere lapdog. The things I have brought to you are some of the rarest items in your realm. The information that I collected for you could be of great benefit to your Majesty. I only ask that I be given the chance to lay out a proposal for the use of said information that I am certain will meet your approval and blessing."

"Silence, toy dog!" Ahuitzotl shouted as he shot up from his throne. His monstrous dog mirrored the master rising to its four feet, growling and frothing at the mouth, ready to attack.

"You do not bark orders in my chambers. Neither requests, proposals, nor pleadings even to save your own life! I am the one and only Huey Tlatoani. Duly elected and revered speaker!" His voice echoed on the walls, magnifying the severity of the tongue lashing directed at me.

"You think you have brought me information that is unknown to me? I am all-knowing, all-seeing! Have you forgotten that I already knew who you were even before I laid eyes on you? I have eyes and ears everywhere, lowly Itzcuintli. Your pochtecatl lords haven't flayed you alive because I have a hand in everything that happens in this realm. I was curious about you. My sources told me that you make moves. That you align yourself with people higher in rank than you and that you always manage to rise in the ranks, something that your handlers do not particularly like. But since you kept bringing rare commodities, and their fat bellies kept engorging with riches, they let have free rein with only minor slaps on the wrist when you step out of line. And you often do so. A man like that can be a great asset or a huge liability for those above him. So, my only question is, which are you? An asset or a liability to me?"

"An asset, your highness. I assure you that I would be an asset to you. I only seek to serve you and the empire, Majesty."

"You think I am simple-minded, Itzcuintli? I didn't come to occupy this throne by being gullible. I know the nature of people. And I know that sometimes, the ones who break the rules for a higher purpose usually end up betraying that high purpose for an even higher one: themselves."

"With all due respect, Revered Speaker. I would never—"

"You will have the audience that you seek with me and then you will lay out the full breath of your proposal. If I find that it is of use to me you will be granted a position among my advisors..."

"Thank you. Thank you, highness. You will not regret it," I replied with a sigh of relief.

"I am not done! That audience will constitute the second of two tests of worth for the position which you could occupy in our realm. The first test will be on the gladiatorial ring against two of my most accomplished warriors and Xolo Ahuitzotl here," he said momentarily glancing over at the rabid dog still seething with rage as it stared me down.

He then looked back up at me and continued saying, "After all...you didn't think you would come out of this unscathed when you unlawfully circumvented your pochtecatl lords to gain this audience with your Tlatoani, did you?"

"But your majesty, although I do know how to defend myself, I am not a warrior. I am pochtecatl. I was never formally trained in the martial arts."

"Very well then, you have two choices. Take the challenge presented here, or I personally deliver you to the pochtecatl headquarters...in pieces! Take your pick."

Tlatoani Ahuitzotl's face suddenly seemed to be overshadowed by a dark cloud that hovered solely about his head. Only the glare of his eyes was visible. His gnawing teeth, like those of his dog next to him, seemed ready to tear me apart, ripping my heart out to eat it as I lay dying, watching in terror...

****

TO BE CONTINUED IN BOOK 2

THE X SERIES

For updates on the next publication date visit

gabrielhugo.com

Addendum

Tenochtitlan is a marked city. The city in the middle of the lake at the center of the Earth is doomed. This is the island city that like the heart of a giant beast pumps life into the first superpower of the Americas. Who has toppled the greatest warriors--the Aztecs? Who has dared challenge the foundations of the heavens? How did an empire of millions of people fall to a small, ragtag band of rogue Spaniards? It didn't. The fall of an empire needs not the intervention of barbarian invaders whether or not they are well-armed with superior weapons, or civilization-ending diseases. The fall of an empire is often the result of the people's will to seek a change in the course of their lives and destiny. By 1492, the time for that change had come to Mexico not from without, but from within. Yet, coincidentally, it arrived simultaneously with strange new people appearing on the horizon of the American hemisphere from the East. Their role in the fate of the old Aztec world order would be determined by a new breed of Mexica (Aztec) political actors. One man among the new breed of Mexica youth realized that in order to live in a different world, an ideal world, one must be willing to be the force that brings about that change. His name was Tonali...a.k.a. "Ali".

Tenochtitlan Must Fall is the first book in the collection in which Ali is introduced. The story starts in the formative years of the protagonist's life but is narrated in part through his dreams, for at 19 years of age, he is already a grown man. In this installment, Ali has been convalescing after having been put to an arduous test in the gladiatorial ring by the fearsome Huey Tlatoani (Emperor) Ahuitzotl in spite of the fact that Ali was not a warrior but a merchant or "pochtecatl". (The details regarding this incident and the Tlatoani's motivations will not become apparent until future installments in the series.) For this and other reasons, Ali is driven by a desire for revenge to destroy the corruption that he would become immersed in as a servant to the elites of Tenochtitlan. Nevertheless, the extent to which his efforts to change his world succeed surpasses his wildest expectations...perhaps not for the better.

The X *Series* is a collection of novellas about the fall of Tenochtitlan and the greater Aztec realm. However, this account is not taken from the point of view of the so-called "conquistadors", nor is it from the viewpoint of conquered and defeated people, like the book by Miguel León Portilla titled "The Broken Spears: The Aztec Account of the Conquest of Mexico".

The X Series is a retelling of true historical events from an alternative perspective. The series' aim is to put an end to long-held fabrications about the end of Mexica rule, one book installment at a time. The official historical record to date has given the world a heavily skewed and fictional set of stories which generally favor the Spanish invaders. And the stories told about the conquest have been passed on generation after generation as true history in an effort to silence competing versions of events of that particular Mexican past. The books in *The X Series* aim to correct the record by sheer common sense, intuition, and better storytelling. These stories are told in a fictional setting with fictional characters, but based on actual events.

About the X

X is the symbol of change. It can represent the symbol of death and the symbol of ambiguity or formlessness, and therefore, fluidity. In popular culture, artistic representations of the dead in cartoons are often drawn with an X in the place of each of the eyes to signal that they are dead. In mathematics, one often hears educators state phrases like "If $4 - X = 3$, what is the value of X?" When the answer to the question is incorrect, the educator will mark the incorrect response with an X to represent a rejection of it. This gives the X the incredible flexibility of transforming from one value to another depending on the question or the problem being posed, and at the same time being the mark or the force that can cancel itself if its present manifestation is an error.

In pre-Hispanic Mesoamerica, the deity "Xolotl" was at times represented with a pair of lines crisscrossed in the form of an X. However, because the Mesoamerican written languages never used the Latin alphabet, it could not have represented that specific letter. But it is curious that that symbol which looks like the letter X would be used in representations of this deity who is known as "the master transformer". Furthermore, here on the Earth plane, Xolotl was represented by two beings who are particular only to Mexico: the Axolotl (a salamander living in the water fulltime) and the Xoloitzcuintli (the Mexican hairless dog, who is said to accompany people through the underworld or Mictlan). Xolotl, therefore, is the guide to the afterlife, which makes sense, since it is a role most befitting a master transformer to help humans transfer from the physical realm to the spirit realm. Curiously, there is a myth about this deity that when the fifth sun was being created, the gods were required to sacrifice themselves to give life to the current era. Xolotl refused to "cancel himself" (as stated above) or sacrifice himself, choosing instead to flee for his life and seek refuge by transforming into different beings. He was eventually found and forced to self-sacrifice. In later installments in this series, the X will come to represent justice, being used on the wicked who have been marked for death...

Glossary of Nahuatl Terms

<u>Common Words</u>

Nantli: Mother

Tajtli: Father

Pochtecatl: Traveling Merchants

Xoloitzcuintli: Ancient rare Mexican dog breed

Cactli: Shoes/sandals

Tlaxkalli: Tortillas

Mexica: Mexican people; from Tenochtitlan

Telpochcalli: Ancient Aztec/Mexica military and trade school for young people

Calmecac: A school for the children of the elite and noble classes in ancient Aztec/Mexica society

Huey Teocalli: The Great Pyramid in Tenochtitlan

Chinampa: Floating crop fields

Chicunamictlan: The final level of the Mictlan afterlife journey

Ahuacatl: Avocado

Chichimeca: Inhabitants in northern territories of Mesoamerica outside the realm of the Aztec/Mexica

Calpulli: Local government; district

Cemitqui: Politician

Atolli: Hot corn & masa beverage; porridge

Xochiquetzal: Aztec goddess of love, art, beauty, and flowers

Wuehxolotl: Turkey

Conetl: Child; boy or girl

Tlaloc: Aztec rain deity

Ahuacatl: Avacado

Mictlan: Underworld of Aztec afterlife

Tenochca: People of Tenochtitlan; Mexica; Aztec

Huey Tlatoani: Revered Speaker; Ruler of the Mexica, the Triple Alliance, and their domain

Huipil: Traditional garment worn by women in Central Mexico

Nahuatl Names

Tonali: Destiny

Ahuiliztli: Joy

Ohtli: Road

Amoxtli: Book

Chimalli: Shield

Moyolehuani: Love; in love

Ahuitzotl: Watering dog (name of actual eighth ruler of the Aztec empire)

Place Names in Aztec times

Tenochtitlan: Capital city of the Aztec Empire; Modern day Mexico City

Tlacopan: Modern day Tacuba in Mexico City

Mazatzintamalco: ancient Tenochtitlan suburb

Chapultepec: Means "Grasshoper Hill;" Located in outskirts of Tenochtitlan; was used as a retreat for Kings and Rulers.

Tlatelolco: Sister city to Tenochtitlan; site of the largest marketplace in the ancient world

Totonacapan: Area where the Totonaca people ruled; modern day Veracruz & Puebla

Popocatepetl: 2nd highest volcano in Mexico located southeast of Tenochtitlan

Gabriel Hugo is one of the latest manifestations of Xolotl, "the master transformer". In this form he has been a film maker, actor, script writer, educator, therapist, translator, publisher, artist, designer, arts promoter, poet, and author of fiction. His latest works are "The Martian Ones: Tales of Human Folly" and "The X Series."

Find more info about Gabriel Hugo at:
gabrielhugo.com

About Xanath Caraza:

Xánath Caraza is a traveler, educator, poet and short story writer. She writes for La Bloga, Smithsonian Latino Center, Seattle Escribe and Revista Literaria Monolito. For the 2018 International Latino Book Awards, she received First Place for Lágrima roja and Sin preámbulos/Without Preamble for "Best Book of Poetry in Spanish" and "Best Book Bilingual Poetry". Syllables of Wind received the 2015 International Book Award for Poetry. Her books of verse Where the Light is Violet, Black Ink, Ocelocíhuatl, Conjuro and her book of short fiction What the Tide Brings have won national and international recognition. Her other books of poetry are Hudson, Le sillabe del vento, Noche de colibríes, Corazón pintado, and her second short story collection, Metztli.